PESHI

Facing Death

ALEX PINESCHI

Copyright © 2020 Alessandro Pineschi

All rights reserved.

This book is dedicated to my mother, who passed away shortly before my definitive return from Iraq. And to my friend Emanuele and all the Peshmerga Warriors of the present, past, and future.

This book is inspired by real events. It is told through the author's experiences, which he has recalled to the best of his ability. Any similarities to trademarks or people, living or deceased, are purely coincidental.

INDEX

Chapter 1 The Fall of Kirkuk

Chapter 2 The March

Chapter 3 The Awakening

Chapter 4 Basheer

Chapter 5 Setup in Kirkuk

Chapter 6 The Child of Mosul

Chapter 7 Conclusion

Chapter 8 The Ten Rules

PREFACE

During the Islamic State's incursion into northern Iraq in 2014, a stream of western volunteers found their way into the ranks of the Kurdish forces known as the Peshmerga. They came from a variety of countries, with an even more variety of backgrounds. Some were horrified by the acts of barbarism carried out by the Islamic State militants and went to support the Kurds in fighting them back. Others were opportunists and saw a quick and easy way to earn fame and profit.

The Kurds, having some common sense, would rarely allow the westerners, many without any military background whatsoever, on the frontlines, let alone take part in operations. A few however, perhaps a handful only, managed to surpass the obstacles that were presented by the Kurds and found themselves in front of the war against the Islamic State, the most savage terrorist organization the world has ever seen. Alex was one of these few volunteers.

Being in a position where I met and worked with a lot of western volunteers, I quickly came to learn that Alex was one of the most professional and capable amongst us. Not only had he a heartfelt sympathy for the Kurds and their cause, but he also had a drive and ambitions that stemmed from his unique warrior mindset. Alex wanted to leave a mark in history, and those of us who know him and his work would say he managed to do so. But at what cost? This book might give some insight into the sacrifices that have to be made by someone who wants to make a difference in this cutthroat part of the world.

Mike Peshmerganor, Author of the Book :
"Blood Makes the Grass Grow"
A Norwegian Volunteer's War Against the Islamic State

1

THE FALL OF KIRKUK

October 16, 2017- Kirkuk Province

It was nighttime and the Tel Ward front was an imperceptible line that cut the Kurdish territories from the Arab ones. After the last few nights spent at the front monitoring the movements of the Shiite militias, the soldiers had not slept for a long time. We were all worried about what the Hash Al-Shaabi's entry into the city with the support of Iraqi forces might mean.

The order from our superiors was to not fight and let them take possession of the objectives they had previously agreed on with our political leaders. There were agreements between the political faction of the Patriotic Union of Kurdistan (PUK) and Baghdad. Our station was the Tel Ward front line, commanded by General Mohammed. We had participated with the soldiers in that offensive and had fought hard to take possession of those territories. We kept an eye on them, as they did with us. It was unbelievable that a few months earlier we had fought together for the same goal and now we were facing each other.

There had already been turbulence between the Kurds and the Shiites and, perhaps that area would have witnessed the explosion of the ethnic tensions.

The Shiites were numerous, organized, and well-armed. If the order ever came to resist their assault, they would have shattered us in the first wave. They possessed over five hundred vehicles, artillery, and thousands of men. An imposing hostile assemblage. Now I can imagine how a German soldier might have felt on the morning of the Normandy landings.

These were moments full of apprehension and tension, and all the soldiers were wondering what would happen to them, to the city of Kirkuk, to their families, to us...

Airports had been closed as well as land borders. Iraq, Iran, and Turkey had closed their borders and were not allowing anyone to leave the country. During the crisis of the referendum, various oil pipelines were closed and the autonomous region of Kurdistan remained isolated, even from a commercial point of view. If I had wanted to leave the country, I would have been forced to travel through Baghdad International Airport with a Visa, which would have led the Iraqis to investigate me. Later on, I found out that there would not be any problem but at the time, it didn't seem like a brilliant idea.

I had fought with the Peshmerga for years. We fought for Kirkuk against the terrorists. It all happened so fast. The war against ISIS was not officially over yet. The referendum for the independence of Kurdistan had taken place and within a short time, allies and enemies had reversed roles. The various embassies issued bulletins inviting their compatriots to leave the country, but it all happened swiftly.

I was serving at the front and often couldn't connect to the internet. And even if I could understand the situation, how could I leave my contingent? *Could I, amid a crisis, abandon everything and everyone?* I did not jump aboard the last plane to Europe and, consequently, I lost the opportunity to save myself in time from the hell that would have broken out shortly after.

Everything will work out, I kept telling myself. *They will find a solution. We are in 2017... these things no longer happen. We are the Peshmerga. The whole world supports us. Kirkuk is ours. We have defended it for years!*

Unfortunately, I was totally wrong. The US sided with the central government of Baghdad, which ordered its troops to take control of Kirkuk. What worried me was not the Iraqi regular forces, but the Shiite militias. A new civil war was upon us.

Under the commanders' orders, we left our front line and. When we arrived back at the base, the tension was already so heavy it could be cut with a knife. We knew that the Shiite militias were pushing and gradually taking control of their pre-established objectives. Many civilians and paramilitary groups took to the streets with the idea of fighting alongside various factions, unaware of the agreements that the government had made with Iraq to avoid unnecessary bloodshed.

The Iraqi army broke through the defense of the Kurdish irregular units like a wave demolishing a sandcastle. Other wild groups instead attacked the Peshmerga, who were ordered to depart. The various Kurdish militias were neither ready nor equipped to face a ground assault of that magnitude on a tactical or strategic level. Moreover, the Kurds were further divided into different factions with different and uncoordinated objectives. This annihilated any possibility of coordination and defense.

Many units fell unnecessarily, refusing to leave their positions without the knowledge of the political agreements made between the parties. Many civilians and volunteers died without understanding what they were fighting for. Chaos broke out in the city. Some paramilitary groups attacked Peshmerga of different factions, accusing them of escaping without even fighting. Barracks and buildings were stormed and looted by groups of irregular fighters, who often triggered senseless conflicts.

With our handful of light vehicles, we were in the thick of the confusion. The irregular groups had set up checkpoints to block the departing traffic. They even tried to block us in, but it didn't work. On the way back to the base, the irregular units attacked us to take over our vehicles and steal our weapons. We fought against the same people we had protected for years. The people whom many of us had sacrificed for.

The convoy passed through the main streets. Flames and smoke rose into the sky, and many civilians were on the street trying to escape from the mayhem. Some shots hit us, perhaps fired from the rooftops. We looked at each other with wide eyes. No one had yet entered Kirkuk. Neither the Iraq Army nor the Shia militias. So who could be firing at us? I asked my men.

"Civil and irregular, Alex..." was their reply.

"And why are they shooting at us!?" I shouted to Salar.

"Because we're running away. They want our weapons, too!"

My vehicle was targeted by bullets from the upper floors of nearby houses. I could hear the impacts on the hood of the GMC. If they wanted to kill us, they would be shooting at the windshield and not at the hood. Did they want to stop us? Or were they just numb-nuts unable to aim? The PKM machine guns mounted on the caissons returned fire, but without pointing at the windows since we didn't want to kill anyone. The message, however, had to be clear: Get off our backs!

We arrived at the base near the headquarters of the PUK political party and saw many military vehicles positioned behind the complex walls. Inside the government building, it was a total mess. Our base was located north of Kirkuk and from our positions, we could see an endless queue of civilian refugees leaving the city. It was an apocalyptic scene. The only escape routes to leave that hell were the road to Sulaimanya and the road to Erbil. Amidst the chaos, I looked for my High Command. Both commanders spoke into two or three telephones simultaneously. I perceived that the situation was getting worse. Information was scarce and the sources unreliable, but from what I could understand, the agreements had not been respected. The Shiites were not stopping at the established objectives but were penetrating the City of Kirkuk. From my contacts, I had learned that the airport and the K1 Air Base had been taken by Iraqi special forces while the Shiite militias were entering the city. *Alex, go away,* I thought to myself. *There is nothing you can do. Politics has already decided. Get out of here...*

I grabbed my commander by the arm and looked him straight in the eye.

"Orders Captain!" I said. "I need orders. Tell me what to do!"

The officer resolutely told me not to worry. That everything would be resolved. That there were political agreements and no one would attack us.

"There was also an agreement that they should have stopped outside Kirkuk!" I said, outraged. "I'm not worried."

Actually, I was terribly worried.

"I'm asking you what to do with my Platoon, Captain!" I said.

The captain nodded to Lieutenant Mariwan and whispered something.

After that, Mariwan took my arm and walked me out of the room. We stopped in front of a window.

"Do you see that over there?" He pointed to an overpass that overlooked the Kirkuk Road, the one that led north towards Erbil "If we lose that junction, no one will be able to leave Kirkuk."

"Are you asking me to hold that bridge?"

"Yes. Take your platoon and see what you can do. And if it turns out to be too hard...abandon your position."

"Okay, Mariwan," I replied tentatively.

"Soresh!!!" I still remember the tone he usually used to call me by my name in Kurdish, Soresh, which means Revolution.

"What?" I replied, upset.

"If you cannot hold the position, go away, okay? Do you understand? Do not engage any regular Iraqi army units or Shiite militias. Just the irregular ones."

"Okay, Mariwan."

I ran toward the square where the boys were freshening up. They too were attached to their phones. (The Kurds always have at least two phones each.) I took Salar, my deputy commander, aside and explained the orders. We gathered everyone and I told them to get ready for a new mission. Salar then called the boys and explained what they should do. The boys did not seem in the mood to go back out there. They were worried about their families.

"It is madness! What are we going to do out there?" Aram asked nervously.

Salar took him aside and shouted in his face, "These are the orders! And we honor them!"

"We have no hope. They will sweep us away! What can we do? We are little more than a dozen men!" said Hardy, who had been aloof until then. Everyone started screaming and arguing with each other. Turmoil was about to break loose.

"GUYS! Listen to me!" I shouted with all my might. When I had their attention, I addressed them with resolution.

"I know we are in a challenging situation. I know you are worried about your families over there. I also understand we have little hope. But if the gangs of irregular people/civilians take control of that street," I pointed to it with my hand, "hundreds of people will not be able to leave Kirkuk and will find themselves amid the crossfire of the fighting." When I was done speaking, I climbed to the roof of the base where I saw hundreds of cars blocking the road in an attempt to leave the hell. It was a scene I will never forget: Cars overloaded with furniture and people, crowded trucks, and the pale color that haunted nearly all their faces. A long, white snake of metal sheets, unable to move forward.

I got the attention of my men. "Look! What do you think will happen when they enter the city? Your families are probably in those cars. We must resist and defend that junction as long as we can. I promise you, once the civilians exfiltrate, we will depart. They are bands of irregulars. They are not really trained soldiers, okay?" I searched their eyes for approval. I got off the roof and approached Aram.

"Hey, are you all right?"

"No, *Mamosta*." Aram was the youngest of the platoon. He had a little girl named Alina and he always came by my quarters to show me videos of his daughter. He was a father before he was a soldier. One day, when I asked him why he had volunteered for Task Force Black, he confessed that he had done it for her, for his baby Alina. Now he feared making his daughter an orphan.

"Look, I got you. Let's do what we can, okay? Come on, let's go!" I said.

I looked for Salar and when I saw him, I ordered, "Bring all the equipment you have. Don't forget the water! And the ammunition!"

"Okay, *Mamosta*!" *Mamosta*. It meant "teacher" in Kurdish. They had called me that for years, ever since I started training them.

We got into the vehicles. I changed the batteries on the radio and turned on the camera to record what might have been my last message.

We were about to throw ourselves into turmoil, without assurances. I vividly remember going through the door of the base. It was black and massive with our panther drawn on it. Humed, my driver, was yelling into the phone. He was speaking to his family members who were leaving Kirkuk.

"Go away! Leave Kirkuk!" he urged them.

I sent a message to Sam, who was flying over Kirkuk with his drone. He asked me where I was and reported that movements were coming into my sector. Sam was part of the US contingent in the area. I had become friends with him and he helped me when he could by giving me information taken from US surveillance drones flying incessantly over the area. We constantly spoke via chat.

"Did you not leave Kirkuk, Alex?"

"No, I did not!"

"I advise you to move as soon as possible."

"Okay, I'll try. Tell me what you see near my position."

"The road to Sulymany is blocked. Yours remains the last open way to leave the city."

We had to protect the road junction from irregular militias and armed gangs who were trying to block escaping civilians. That was the only way out of

Kirkuk and whoever took control of that road would halt those who didn't want to be in that hell. I don't know why the irregulars wanted to control that road. Perhaps they planned to get weapons to all the Peshmerga units that had been ordered to depart.

With a handful of vehicles, we went out to garrison the area. There was so much confusion; the orders were not clear. What were we to do if the Iraqi Army arrived? My mission remained the same: defend a motorway junction from illegal gangs. We took our positions on the bridge that crossed the main road connecting Kirkuk to Erbil. Below us, hundreds of vehicles carrying fleeing civilians were trying to escape.

We parked our Hummers on the sides of the bridge, leaving space for the runaway cars to pass. I arranged our vehicles to cover 360 degrees around us with the heavy machine guns, then disembarked the snipers and put them in position on both sides. I had some RPG rocket launchers and AT4s with me, plus we had our PKMs. We could hold the position if the irregulars attempted an assault.

It was only a matter of seconds before the hostilities began.

Some small arms bullets fell on us. We immediately went to cover, trying to identify the source. It was hard because everyone was firing and we could hear shots coming from everywhere. At that point, I shouted to Salar, "Don't shoot! Confirm who you are engaging!"

Every time I peeked over the edge of the vehicle I was using as cover, I heard the sharp snap of a bullet as it passed me. We returned fire sporadically, as we were unable to identify the attackers. We just knew that they were always shooting from different locations. The civilian vehicles gradually began to dwindle and the fire toward our position became more and more intense. We were now under attack from several fronts simultaneously. We managed to spot some irregular troops that tried to approach us from the open ground of the bridge's slope. With a few well-placed shots, they were neutralized or forced to flee. The minutes began to pass incessantly and I lost track of time.

We held our position on that bridge, pushing back those who tried to take control of it. Some RPGs caught up with us, detonating dangerously close to our position as the Hummer tires exploded and the vehicles were riddled with bullets. We had been passive targets for too long.

"Let's get out of here! The civilians have now fled!" someone shouted.

"Hold your position!" I ordered in a powerful voice to be heard over the sound of the blows. "There are still some cars missing. Over there, near the statue!" Yes, the statue of the Kurdish fighters. There it was, concrete-colored and about ten meters high, overlooking one of the arteries with an indifferent pose. A Kurdish soldier in traditional clothing holding an AK relaxed on his shoulder. At the moment, it seemed to be a monument of defeat rather than a product created to remember the heroes of the past.

Salar joined me, out of breath.

"*Mamosta*, we are all concerned. We have almost run out of ammunition, the vehicles are destroyed, and the Shiites are arriving. They will kill us. We have done our duty. Now we have to go."

Sam wrote to me that some military vehicles were on their way to our position. They were hostile militias for sure. I tried to reach Mariwan on the radio channel to tell him that with damaged vehicles and no ammunition, I wanted to fall back to our base. I succeeded on the second attempt. The answer was categorical and shouted into the microphone:

"KEEP YOUR POSITION! The captain's orders are to stay there!"

The scenario became surreal. The flow of cars decreased and the four-lane road became more and more deserted. Who were we supposed to protect now?

The fire of the irregular troops intensified until it no longer allowed us to leave cover to return fire. I called Mariwan again.

"Listen, I'll stay here if you want, but we have run out of ammunition, the vehicles are destroyed, and I have a couple of wounded men. Plus, no more civilians are driving by. I'll stay here with Salar, but send me relief for my men!"

"Wait, Soresh. I have to ask the captain."

While I waited, we responded to the attacking fire while trying not to waste ammo. Peshraw, with his PKM, fired single shots, changing positions after each shot. Dler was grazed and I had Dlshad on the ground, shot in the leg. The situation was escalating too fast.

"Soresh! The captain says to get out of there! Immediately!" When I heard those words, I wanted to bite the microphone.

"I told you that ten minutes ago! Roger! But my vehicles cannot move! Send a pick-up to get us! Now!"

"Okay, Soresh!" I ended the call and looked around to plan the retreat.

"Salar! Get the men rearranged! They are picking us up now! Recover everything you can from the vehicles!"

Mariwan called me back after a moment.

"Soresh, don't abandon the vehicles. I repeat, the captain says NOT to abandon the Hummers!" I swung my head in disbelief.

"Mariwan, the vehicles cannot move!" I replied angrily. "The tires are in pieces!" At the same time, a new message from Sam also arrived: *Military vehicles approaching your position. Get out of there, Alex!*

I tried to remove myself from the situation and organize my thoughts. *Okay… okay… Alex, think… Quickly, but think! Make order… and make a fucking decision!* I decided to recover the vehicles. Even with flat tires, somehow the engines still worked and they could drive. I tried to cheer up my men.

"Guys, let's try to recover the vehicles. They are a few hundred meters from the base." I ordered that only drivers could stay in the Hummers in an attempt to trudge them to the base. The rest of the platoon and I opted to walk back and cover each other, making a jerky advance to the base.

Somehow, we reached the base. The guard at the driveway entrance opened the door in a hurry. Some armed men came out to cover our entrance. Within minutes, the irregular troops took up the positions we had abandoned on the bridge and began targeting the base, firing directly into the courtyard of the military facility. The shots bounced around the rooms like pinballs. We had no escape and could not organize an effective defense. We realized that the only way to survive was to abandon the base. The militias had various types of military weapons and the vehicles in their possession still had the symbol of the stolen Peshmerga units.

The base was now semi-deserted. Most of the vehicles were gone, and the rooms were empty. Many had retreated to Command, while some had escaped in their own private cars.

It was a surreal situation that I was struggling to understand. *Did they leave us here? Where is everyone?* I called Mariwan again.

"Hey! We're back! Where have they all gone?"

"Soresh... We retreated to the generals' quarters behind the Command. Come. They won't have the courage to enter here!" Once again, I found it hard to believe my ears.

"Have you left our base to stand in defense of the generals' quarters?!" I yelled into the microphone.

"Alex, these are the orders... I'm sorry."

I was furious. Disappointed. Embittered and destroyed. *I'm not going to die to protect any fucking general or political leader!* I thought. *My war stops here. From now on, I will think just for myself and my boys.*

Shots were bouncing off the walls of the complex and some broke the windows. The door was closed and a Hummer had been placed against it to reinforce it. We had barricaded ourselves inside, but we could not see anything and we had no visibility of the outside. We didn't know what was happening out there. *I have to understand what is happening beyond the walls!*

I looked at the command terrace, which was about three hundred meters away from our base. I tried to figure out if it was feasible to reach it. I would have to run about three hundred meters through the parking lot in the open, exposed to enemy fire, until I reached the entrance door of Command. I took a breath, summoned some courage, and got ready to run. I checked my combat gear, the helmet, and my weapon. I was ready. My men sensed my intentions and said, "Where are you going? Stay here. They won't come in here. And if they do, we'll fight. We will defeat them." Honestly, at that moment, I pondered the situation. Could we withstand an attack of illegals? Yes, maybe we could. But we certainly could not counter an attack by the Shiite militias. If they reached the base, they would enter without a doubt. And what would they do to us? *What would they do to me?*

I was a foreigner. Shiite militias used to burn the US flag and proclaim themselves fierce enemies of the West. And I was a Westerner fighting with the Peshmerga, which was one of the top reasons to get killed by them. The first moments of any invasion or offensive come to my mind. There is no order, no law. Whoever loses is in the hands of the winners. Without protections. Without rights.

I *had* to get out of Kirkuk as quickly as possible. I found my courage and took a breath. I braced myself to sprint to the door. Shots bounced off the parking lot, possibly fired from the rooftops of surrounding houses. Who knows? It was a total bloody mess. *Three... two... one... GO!*

I ran with my heart between my teeth as if Satan himself were chasing me. I wished it was only Satan. I tried to ignore the sound of gunfire around me. Stride after stride, my eyes focused solely on my goal. I reached the door, accompanied by the cheers of the men who were watching me from the square. I caught my breath, taking in large gulps of air, and took up my weapon.

I opened the door. Empty rooms. After a while, I found the terrified Nepalese workers hiding inside the kitchens of the complex.

"We are afraid," they kept telling me.

I tried to reassure them in English. "Don't worry, they won't do anything to you. They're not looking for you. At worst, they'll make you work without paying you." I left them, but they were not convinced by my words. I ran up the stairs and found the building totally empty. The equipment was starting to feel damn heavy from running up all the steps.

I went up to the upper floor. I had finally reached the terrace! I looked beyond the walls of the base.

It was shocking.

Over fifty vehicles of various types, mostly pick-up vehicles, had surrounded the base. The reason? The base was inside the Kirkuk political party complex, and the irregulars were angry. On national TV, under the control of the PDK, they said that the Peshmerga of the PUK had left their position without a fight and the Shiite militias were entering. The anger of the city was thrown at us, the security unit of the political complex of the PUK.

I saw the base get surrounded while everything was collapsing. Kirkuk, Task Force Black, my Team… And I… I was screwed. I no longer had a chain of command, there were no more orders, and the enemy was at the gates. Literally. I realized that it was likely the end of my life. *Why didn't I get on that goddamn last plane?*

If they had entered, perhaps they wouldn't have killed me immediately. Or maybe they would have tortured me in front of a video camera to send a crystal-clear message to those who thought to help the Kurds. Would the Kurds have defended me? Perhaps they would hand me over to the Shiites themselves in exchange for some of their generals.

Everything slowed down. I was lucid, as I had been just a few other times in my life. I entered a kind of sensory bubble. The universe around me ceased to exist. I put my hand on the holster of my Glock and stroked the retention lever with my thumb. I did so slowly. With my palm, I touched the handle and felt every protrusion of the gun with extreme sensitivity. I increased the pressure on the release device and slowly took the weapon out of the holster. Chaos was outside, but I isolated myself in a world where everything was muffled and slowed down. I brought the gun in front of me, lowered my eyes, and looked at it. I could see every detail, every engraving on the slide, every slightest knurling on the handle. I put my hand on the slide. I pulled it back and the bullet went into the barrel. I didn't think about it. I just did it. I stared at the serial number of my weapon stamped on the single metal strip embedded in the polymer of the lower frame: *HBS 432 Glock 19 Austria.*

Did I really want to shoot myself in the head? Did I really want to die reading *HBS 432 Glock 19 Austria*?

I raised my eyes as if looking for hope, but in the horizon of the mess, among the flames and smoke, shots and screams... I found something. Something stronger than any hope. A promise. A promise I had made.

I quickly came back to my senses. *What the hell is going through my head!?* Then I saw her again, in another time and another place.

"Ale, look me in the eye. Will you promise me that you will do everything to get home?" my mother's voice is serious, worried.

"Yes, mom." I replied, "I promise you."

I promised.

I ran down the stairs, across the open parking lot again, playing dice again with death. I rounded up my boys. I took a breath and finally declared:

"I have to get away from here..."

"It was time! Did you wake up just now?" Peshraw commented aloud. I spread my arms and shook my head as if to justify myself.

"Guys, get me out of Kirkuk. We will use my service car."

"What were you waiting for? It was time for you to make a move! We'll take you away from here," another said.

We reached the vehicle, but some of the boys did not want to leave Kirkuk. They wanted to stay to fight and defend it.

"Go, Alex," they said to me. "Save yourself. Because whoever catches you won't be kind to you..."

Three other men and I jumped aboard. Fortunately, I always had an escape kit ready in my personal vehicle. The kit consisted of:

- A main tank of one hundred and twenty liters of fuel, which was always full
- An additional twenty-liter auxiliary tank

- A water tank of about twenty liters with ten liters of drinking water
- An ammunition box of 800-round for the M4 carbine
- An AK-47 with five magazines
- An escape/bug out backpack
- A solar panel plus several power banks
- Comfort items and combat rations
- Repair kits and tools for the vehicle
- A radio
- A fair amount of cash
- Spare civilian and military clothes

There was no time left. I had to escape from that hell. I started talking to myself. *What are you going to do, Alex? First, let's get out of here, then we'll go north. We have a civilian vehicle and we won't be too conspicuous, and if they try to stop us... well... we'll do what we are able to do.*

After the quick and overly optimistic briefing with myself, I turned back to my boys.

"Take me out of the city center, then I'll make it somehow."

We went out through the back door usually intended for garbage and provisioning vans, which led into a small side street. The base was located in the northern part of the city, and it was easy to leave the urban area and reach the suburbs.

We drove for about twenty minutes, looking at the digital map of my PDA when finally, we reached a well-isolated area.

I stopped the vehicle and decided that it was the right time and place to plan the next step. My boys wanted to go back to their families in Kirkuk. They were worried about them. It was understandable, and if we had run into the other faction of Peshmerga, things could have taken a bad turn. On my own, I had more chances of going unnoticed and, in case of contact, I could pass myself off as a runaway foreigner. I decided to leave the vehicle with them and continue marching north and reach the border of the governorate. I explained my intentions to my fellow soldiers. After a moment of silence, the first comment came.

"I mean, let me understand…" one of them replied. "Are you telling us that we must leave you here, alone in the void and that you will go to Erbil on foot?" His words exuded skepticism. I spread my arms.

"Well, yes, more or less..." and I gave him my cheekiest smile.

Peshraw told me that he had a trusted contact, a relative like an uncle or something, who lived in the village on the northern border between Kirkuk and Erbil Governorate. He would help me cross the border safely. He told me to contact him as soon as I was near the village and that he would pick me up near the village bridge. We identified the pre-arranged rendezvous point on the map. Peshraw called this elusive trusted relative without giving specific information and limited himself to asking him only the situation in his village on the border. Sometimes, you just have to trust and hope in the circumstances. They say hope is not a good plan, but if you have a good plan, you also have hope.

"Okay," I said. "I can't do otherwise and you can't come with me. Plus, if I use the car I risk being more visible because the villages are controlled by the irregulars."

The boys looked at each other as if wondering if they were doing the right thing by letting me try to escape alone. They had always been very protective in regards to me. I tried to convince them that I could do it alone. Initially, they totally refused the idea of letting me go but, in the logic of events, it was the most sensible thing to do. Chaos reigned in the city. Their families were in the midst of that mess and we had no idea what would happen shortly thereafter.

They looked at me and argued among themselves. I gathered they had conflicting opinions. Peshraw claimed it was wrong to let me go alone. It was best if I hid at his place and waited for things to calm down. Aram, on the other hand, said it was a very bad idea. We had no idea about the intentions of the Shiites. The more time that passed, the harder it would be to get out of Kirkuk. And we didn't know the location of the other irregulars and Peshmerga factions. Anyone could have spotted me and in the collective chaos, a foreigner would have been a good bargaining chip.

Soon, all my boys started yelling at each other for a solution. Around here, those who shout the loudest usually have the most solid arguments. Or so it was believed. I isolated myself from the screams and bickering and planned the route by studying the digital map of my PDA, trying to figure out the possible waypoints where to stop.

I set up a roadmap and standby and, in the meantime, I wrote and poured all the directions into my trusty notebook to have a paper backup of the distance and magnetic orientation data to follow with a compass. I never rely too much on battery-operated gizmos.

"I can do it!" I stated, throwing a fist of satisfaction on the hood of the off-road vehicle "Guys, I can do it! No problem!" I turned to my fellow soldiers

"M'N ASKARYA!" *I am a soldier*!

I looked Peshraw in his now bright eyes, tired from years of wars and from the sleepless nights of the previous days. Silence. I stared at him and spoke to him again, cautiously, as if I had to convince a child of a truth of which even I was not sure.

"Azanem, you Mamosta." *I know, you are my Master*, he replied. Suddenly, Peshraw hugged me impetuously and repeated several times in a low voice: *You... Mamosta.* And he started to cry. I tried to cheer him up. It was hard to get rid of the lump in my throat that was choking me.

Aram looks from the roof of the base at the cars of civilians fleeing Kirkuk

"No worries... I'll do it. Now go, guys. Take my car. And if God wills it, one day, you will give it back to me." I hugged them tightly one by one, aware that perhaps I would never see them again. Now I no longer had a team. I was no longer anyone's concern and no one was under my responsibility. I was alone. And I would face fate with my equipment and my training.

2

THE MARCH

I didn't have many options.

The only way to leave that hell was to march on foot, trying to hide out as much as I could. I developed my itinerary, planning around two main variables. First: follow the morphology of the land. I wanted to walk along the riverbed because it gave me good visual coverage. I considered that the river, being partly drained, could be walked on and could offer a path below ground level to cover me. I considered that there were no roads around the river, so it was hard to intercept onboard vehicles. Then, if I got lucky in some wells, I would have found water. My second strategy was to stay away from all villages and urban centers. Given that the situation was not clear, I should consider anyone hostile.

Thanks to the cartographic software that I had installed on my PDA, I could easily check and see in advance the morphology from the ground, the contour lines, and any details. I had a solar panel with me plus a couple of battery packs, which ensured me a constant energy supply.

I planned everything and dumped the waypoints on both devices to have everything on two digital media devices. Also, my faithful notebook ensured that all the data was in a safe place, considering that it could never be downloaded, broken, or run out. Paper, how cool.

For navigation, I opted to follow the "analog method" and use the digital device just to get the point on the map. I would have tracked the distance with my wrist GPS, a Garmin that my father gave me before I left. The compass I had, on the other hand, was of good quality. It was a heavy model in an oil bath. A good compass should never be missing from a soldier's kit.

I decided to leave around nightfall, taking advantage of the darkness. I also had my night-vision device with me and my infrared laser mounted on the rifle. If I had been forced to fight at night, I would have had the technology to shoot accurately. I threw off my military uniform and put on a pair of olive green trousers and a blue shirt. In case of danger, once I was free of my military gear, I could easily have passed myself off as a journalist or something. At least, I hoped so.

Overall, my planned route was about forty kilometers, mainly on flat terrain in the first part and then hilly for the rest. The territory consisted of rocks and stones. I did not know the weight of the equipment, but it was considerable. Also, I hadn't slept for a couple of days, had an empty stomach, and had been in numerous fights. Surprisingly, I had no appetite. I was anxious. To be honest, I was freaking scared. Scared of not making it, scared of losing myself, scared of being caught and killed. I was afraid of never seeing my friends again and not continuing to do what I loved to do. I was left alone, on foot, and with no support. I could only count on myself, on my training, and, fortunately, I had adequate water and ammunition. I knew what I had to do. I knew how to navigate by following the compass. I knew how to survive in hostile environments and if someone forced me to fight, I had an advantage thanks to an enormous tactical and technological dominance.

This faith gave me the strength to face the circumstances. *I'm trained*, I kept repeating to myself. *I've done this a hundred times. Okay, maybe never in these extreme conditions, but I'm a soldier and now it's time to prove it.* My equipment was quite heavy and bulky. I wanted to keep the helmet light, as it was good to support the PVS 14 night vision device and allowed me to have my hands free to shoot with the PEQ 15 laser illuminator to sight the targets. My principal weapon was the M4A1 carbine equipped with an Aimpoint red-dot sight that also worked in night mode. It was also equipped with additional backup sights and a tactical flashlight mounted on the Picatinny rails. As a secondary weapon, I was carrying my trusty Glock 19 in a holster, also supplied with a tactical flashlight.

I reluctantly decided to get rid of the ballistic plates to be lighter to march and run faster in case of contact with the enemy. *Anyway,* I thought to myself, *if I am wounded in combat, I can't count on medical support. If the plates were to withstand the blows, however, I am doomed anyway. Once in the hands of the enemy with the broken ribs, I would have been on the clock.*

In the front pockets of my combat vest, I carried five M4 magazines of thirty rounds each and on the side pouches, I had a smoke grenade and another fragmentation grenade. On the left shoulder strap, I had fastened the wrist GPS that I used to measure the distance from point to point. Plus, I was holding a tourniquet with an elastic band. In the inside pocket, I had my radio that I turned on during the stops to listen to any communications. The radio was great for intercepting radio broadcasts in the area and I could understand whether or not someone was nearby and, depending on the language spoken, their identity. I could count on a good listening range since I had the whip antenna with me that I had folded meticulously. A headset in the left ear completed the radio system. My combat equipment was based on a belt that I had carefully equipped which included:

- A magazine for the Glock
- An emergency magazine for my M4
- A second first-aid kit
- Multitool pliers
- A spare tourniquet

I removed the back panel of the tactical vest–a kind of flat dorsal backpack–and poured its contents into another small one where I had put four more cartridge tanks for the M4, a smoke grenade, a tablet with complete cartography of the area, a foldable solar panel with a power bank, a spare battery kit, a small repair kit, a laser Range-Finder to measure the distance to any targets, a small flashlight with front connection, four packages of mineral salts, a liter of drinking water, a small butane stove with its water tank, a mini-kit to purify the water, some solid lighter tablets and matches, a couple of cans of tuna, a pack of dried fruit, a pack of almonds, sugar and soluble coffee, ampoules of medicines such as painkillers, antibiotics, cortisone, and tablets, and an 8-ounce bag of saline solution with the relative kit to open venous access.

According to outlining, having to face a weighted march of about forty kilometers, I opted to insert the "evacuation" backpack inside the main one. In case I had to abandon the large backpack to be more agile, I could have easily put on the small one and run away.

I estimated that at night, the temperatures were relatively cold. I decided to pack something in the big backpack to protect myself from the cold: a fleece, a windbreaker, a T-shirt, a pair of spare socks, and a fleece hat. (Blessed be the one who invented the marvel of polyester fabric.)

I also decided to add four 1.5-quart bottles of water. On average, a human needs about two quarts per day, but I had to calculate the waste of energy that would lead me to consume more water. I opted for six quarts to have a guaranteed water supply every day. That way, I could ensure the autonomy of about three days. The idea was also to march at night to avoid the daytime heat and with a bit of luck, I could easily cover the water needs for the duration of the march without having to draw from external sources that could deviate my itinerary or take any risk.

The reasoning is simple: you can have all the equipment in the world, but if you have no water reserves in the field, thirst will kill you, not enemy fire.

That was the end of my checklist. It was time to go.

My men held me in a strong hug, their eyes filled with tears. I had been their commander but they had been my guardian angels and if anything happened to me, they would never forgive themselves. It broke my heart to see them like that.

I knew how tough it was for them to leave me. They got into the car and slowly drove back to that hell of a city. I sat on the rocky ground, leaning on my backpack, waiting for the sunset of that bloody day that would forever mark my life.

I started moving at sunset. I wanted to walk in the dark to be seen. My goal was to reach the village on the border of the Kirkuk governorate and cross the river that divided the border. I had calculated my entire route and I was sure I could easily navigate in that environment.

The evening was cool but, given the pace and weight of the equipment, I felt hot. Physically, I felt fine and I started walking at a fast pace to stabilize it. I slowed my pace and also emotionally calmed down. I convinced myself to enjoy the walk and to experience a one-of-a-kind adventure.

Peshraw had told me not to worry, to take all the time necessary for the journey, and that his uncle would not leave the village. The agreement was that when I arrived near the meeting point, I would send him a message. His uncle would come in his pickup and help me cross the border. Peshraw was a soldier, and he knew what he was talking about and took care of the details. He sent me a picture of his uncle and his pickup: an old Toyota Hilux that had seen better days. We used the same cartographic software to communicate, and then he gave me the MGRS coordinates of the meeting point. The village was on the border, but completely Kurdish. It stood away from the main streets and control checkpoints. A perfect place. Too bad for the forty kilometers I had to travel on foot to get there.

I planned to break the night walk into two sessions and to rest during the day. The ground was mostly rocky and soft at times. I observed the horizon around me. I had come out of a chaotic city of nearly seven hundred and fifty thousand inhabitants, and now I was in the middle of a pebbly desert. If they had told me I was walking on the surface of Mars, I would have almost believed it. I was in the middle of nowhere. And it was starting to get dark for real. I walked, following the compass, and now and then, I stopped to take stock of the situation. I used the phone to navigate offline since I had previously downloaded all the maps of the area. I wanted to avoid connecting to any network as I figured if I turned on the phone, someone could locate me. Today, it seems like a silly thought but at the time, it seemed like brilliant intuition. So the smartphone was in airplane mode the whole time, and I only used it as a digital map. I walked and made stops to listen and check the surrounding environment.

When I had to handle the phone for the paper point, I covered myself with the poncho to avoid being detected by the display light. At night, enemies can spot the light from a smartphone screen several hundred feet away if you're unlucky.

I had planned two different types of stops. The first was short, where I primarily did observation and listening activities. To look around, I used my night vision, which could easily detect a small light source at a great distance. The only lights I could make out were those of some farms miles away. Also, since it was night, I tried to listen to the sounds of the surrounding countryside to identify any kind of movement and activity. The only sounds I heard were the barking of dogs in the distance. I also used my scent. I tried to catch a possible human presence, perhaps the smoke and fire of a bivouac.

After the checks, I drank or nibbled something. I had dried fruit and raisins with me. At each stop, I reminded myself to do something reasonable. To drink adequately, for example, to stay constantly hydrated. It was essential to stay hydrated and eat at every stop because, at any time, I could be forced to leave the backpack and lose all the equipment. In that case, the best thing I could take with me was my body, wholly and entirely. The breaks were short and with planned activities. I took what I needed from my backpack and then immediately set off again.

I had also planned longer stops. They were dedicated to marking the location, observation, identification of possible threats, more hydration, food, and also to rest my body.

Time was on my side and I wanted to avoid killing myself with fatigue and then remaining stationary for hours in one place to recover. I preferred to set a smoother schedule and rest during the ride. That way, I could balance physical work and rest with a greater chance to go further quickly. When I was preparing to make these stops, I made sure to choose a proper place that could somehow give me cover.

During the march, I thought. I wandered with my thoughts. I was thinking about the fact that maybe I shouldn't have stayed in Iraq. I should have got on that damn last flight to get back to Italy right away. I thought about Kirkuk, my boys, my car, and what would become of them all. I walked in total nothingness, thousands of miles away from home, without any assurance. I had no guarantees that Peshraw's uncle was a reliable person. I didn't know if the Kurds of the PDK would treat me like a traitor. I didn't know if, to the Iraqi government, I was a wanted man. I didn't even know if the Kurds in my unit would accuse me of desertion. I did not know if once I returned to Italy, I would find myself in front of a judge to explain what I was doing in the middle of a civil war on the other side of the world. I didn't even know how the people I might meet would behave. Would they try to capture me and sell me to ISIS or Shiites?

I had no certainty except my route to follow. I thought I had made a promise and I had kept it. I didn't run away like all the other volunteers. I had stayed with those who had shared a war. And now I had left my boys. I had left Kirkuk. And it had all happened just a few hours ago.

In the city, it was a slaughterhouse. Everyone against everyone. Factions of Kurds against each other. Armed irregulars on the streets. We tried to protect that bridge till we could allow escaping civilians to leave that hell. We had done what was right to do.

As the march went on, I wondered why? Why? Is the war against ISIS not over yet? We and the Iraqis were allies. Why has chaos broken out today? Why? Why? Many whys. Too many. "Why" would find no answer in the boundless and brilliant starry sky that reigned over me. I walked, step by step, to save my life, and, for the first time, I fought only for myself, just to survive.

Me.

Alone.

From a certain point of view, I felt calmer because I was the architect of my actions and destiny.

The hours passed, and I didn't meet a soul. No news was good news. The only sounds in the distance were the dogs of the farms lost in the territory.

The night was clear and the sky was swarming with stars that were bright and visible in the darkness. Now and then, I got lost staring at the sky, I thought of my platoon, of my boys at the base. I couldn't turn on the phone and had no way of knowing what was going on. It was a terrible feeling.

I checked the batteries of my devices from time to time and recharged them with the power banks. The pace made me sweat, but physically I felt full of energy. At each stop programmed as "long" after the usual checks, I changed my shirt and covered myself with the windproof jacket. When I was still, the night air was damn cold. Once, the brilliant idea of preparing a cup of hot tea crossed my mind. I gave up, calling myself an idiot. I wasn't hiking in the mountains of Liguria. I had to avoid performing activities that could have indicated my position.

I was aware that anyone who found an armed man with military equipment could have reacted in the worst possible way. And if the Kurds had found me, I could not have said I was a member of TASK FORCE BLACK, as the Erbil PDK party national TV had declared my unit as the first to run away without a fight. This news pissed off civilians, who decided to attack our patrols and set fire to several of our vehicles just to remind us that in war, you fight and don't run away.

I was alone, and my only remaining hope was to reach Peshraw's uncle. I studied the map again and confirmed there was no other way to cross the border than through that village. It was the only bridge over the river in the region. Still, I kept planning alternatives in the event "the uncle" did not show up to meet me.

Should I have walked through the houses of a village in combat gear in the middle of the night? Should I ditch all my equipment and walk past, pretending to be a reporter on the run from Kirkuk? I didn't know what kind of controls there were on the border or how I was supposed to behave. What if the Shiites had intended to invade Erbil, too? No, fuck it. It was impossible. The Kurds would never allow it.

I continued my march toward the first checkpoint where I should have stopped and let the day pass, hiding the best I could.

I was not far from my final destination and at a pretty elevated point of my path. I was impressed because the GPS told me I was about seven hundred meters above sea level. I started in Kirkuk, which is about four hundred meters above the sea. Wow, I thought. I had already smashed three hundred meters in altitude.

I looked at the clock: 11:30 p.m., October 16, 2017.

In half an hour, it would be my birthday. And at the same time exactly one year earlier, I was seeking rest on the rocks of the Mosul Desert, fresh from the battle that marked the end of the Caliphate. And I was there, with my Peshmerga. I still remember the words I jokingly said to my friend Sebastiano, author of the documentary *Hunting ISIS*.

"Today, I am thirty-three. Let's try to make it to thirty-four." *I still have that video,* I thought. And here I was on the stroke of my 34th birthday, still fighting to survive until my next one.

I planned to spend the day trying to rest and in an altitude advantage. I would be in a position where I could observe what was happening in the village. I should have found a hole in the rocks and used a camouflage net to conceal my hiding place.

I began to feel the light change and I was still far from my first waypoint. I had been on the road for about fifteen hours and had covered just under fifteen miles. I had at least another nine left and I wanted to take advantage of the last hours of darkness to find a good place for the bivouac. I found a small depression among the rocks where I could hide. However, it gave me no visibility to the outside. But I didn't have anything better available. There were no roads nearby and my position was reachable only on foot by any people who could venture there. Fpr example, shepherds intent on grazing a flock of sheep. But I had already read a similar story in a famous book, and it didn't end well.

According to my plan, I would have to spend the whole day undetected to avoid being seen. The idea of stopping didn't thrill me too much, but I had to stop driving by force. I was tired and hadn't slept in days. I wanted to prepare my bivouac so that I could abandon it at the slightest sign of danger. I wanted to avoid dropping too much material out of the backpack.

No one was on my trail and no one had spotted me. I placed my poncho sheet on the ground by folding it into three parts to make a thin mattress and make the ground more comfortable. I had often slept on naked stones during breaks during assaults, but if there was an opportunity to be comfortable, why not take advantage of it? It would improve my rest quality and, consequently, my following operational yield.

I had to reason, think, make decisions, and plan. I had to take advantage of the hours of rest I had available. Amid those rocks, I realized I could only use my hearing to detect any onlookers.

I put the large backpack between my legs and leaned my back on the small backpack I was wearing. I organized myself by taking the necessary items from the large backpack and kept my rifle on the right, always at hand.

A beautiful sunrise came and I enjoyed the show from the front row. I thought about how I had managed up to that point. I strongly believed that if I had come this far without a scratch, the worst was behind me. My mind kept going back to Kirkuk, Saler, Peshraw, and the people of Kirkuk, Rahimawa, and Shoraw. I was thinking about my base and my unit.

I had escaped. I had filled my mouth with the promise to fight to the end. Instead, I found myself running away on foot in the middle of the desert, leaving everything behind. What would they say about me in Kirkuk? That Mamostà

Shoresh has escaped? What would the friends with whom I had shared a hundred battles say? The trial started in my head, where I was judge and defendant at the same time.

No, it wasn't an escape. I left as a soldier and I tried to get back to my lines. Maybe we will reorganize! Or are they attacking Erbil?

I was confused, but I was sure about one thing: I wanted to survive and I had already come this far. I couldn't give up.

I'll wait for nightfall, I'll rest... No one will ever come here looking for me. There are no roads and around. It's all deserted. Plus, I'm at a high altitude. Relax, Alex, Come on...

I didn't like the idea of being alone and asleep in the desert. It wasn't in a real hiding place. The sun rose in the sky and the night gave way to a new day. A new October 17. I had sweated this birthday. I should be celebrating it! As far as I knew, it could be the last.

I was craving a coffee. I had the mocha in my backpack. Yes, a goddamn mocha in war. I always kept Lavazza coffee in the cartridge belt of my backpack. It may not have been the most tactical thing in the world, but I had what it took to make myself a good coffee. If I had lit a fire, they could have caught me for smoking and caffeine was not the most recommended substance to consume in such situations. Caffeine dehydrates the body and does not allow one to sleep. Tactically, it would have been the wrong thing to do. But, you know what I thought? *After all, it's my birthday… I'll make a damn coffee!* I unscrewed the mocha and poured the water into it up to the level of the valve. I put in the filter and spooned the coffee in. The scent of the powder alone drove me mad with happiness. I didn't press it too hard so as not to make it too strong. In the end, I just wanted coffee to savor it. I opted for the Trangia gel stove to release a flame without making smoke. I looked for a flat surface to place all the stuff on. The sun was rising and my coffee was as well. The mocha made its reassuring mutter, releasing its aroma. It was a beautiful morning, and the coffee was delightful. I tasted it slowly from my plastic cup. I didn't skimp on the sugar. The coffee was my birthday cake.

The darkness would come in twelve hours. I had to try to sleep. I sat on my poncho. It wasn't a five-star mattress, but it was fine. I had previously removed some stones and prepared the ground to be more comfortable. I decided to take off my boots for a while to give my feet some rest, too. I put on my spare socks. The fabric was fresh and felt good. I shouldn't have undressed too much. I took off my vest and lay down, still holding the M4 in my hands. I put my boots back on but did not lace them up again so the blood in my feet could circulate more freely.

The sun was getting very intense and I realized there was too much light. I looked for the glasses in my backpack and, luckily, I found them immediately. The sun's rays hit my face. My eyes were heavy, but falling asleep was a challenge. Too much light, too many thoughts. *I knew I didn't need that coffee,* I thought. *What do I do, sleep? I do not sleep... Dunno, I'll try.* Anyone who appeared to hurt me would have had to deal with my caffeine hit and M4.

Instead, I fell asleep, but it was a troubled sleep. At every noise, I suddenly opened my eyes. It was not a night of real sleep, but a kind of suffered half-sleep. Maybe I dreamed. In those hours of uncertain sleep, my mind began to offer me a series of images, sounds, and sensations. Bizarrely, I found myself thinking about my life, about the whole set of linked events that had brought me from Liguria to laying in the middle of stones in the Iraqi desert during a war.

I thought back to my young self, to that dreamy boy who had grown up in the Canaletto district of La Spezia. My father was a good person who ran an electrical shop in town with dignity. My mother, the light of my life, just wanted me to get at least a diploma. I spent my days on the street with the boys of a neighborhood considered difficult by everyone, where there were few opportunities for redemption and a desire to lead another life. Probably the only district of La Spezia where you couldn't see the sea, but you could simply guess its presence since we were in the shadow of the port facilities. There were few happy faces on the street and many houses that needed some tweaking to be considered decent. I didn't want to study and I didn't have a clear idea of my future. Like all the guys from La Spezia, I had a couple of passions: engines and attempt the Selection to join the Navy Raiders. We used to see them during their exercises in front of Le Grazie and even when they lent themselves in the summer for parachute jumps during some demonstration on the coast.

There was September 11.

I was in my father's shop and on the TV, we saw those images that would change history. At the time, I did not have clear ideas about the various geopolitical alignments in the world, but I decided that I had to do something. I told my father that I would drop out of school and seek a military career. His response was succinct:

"You are a dickhead. That's all I have to say"

Nonetheless, I still showed up for the Navy eligibility visit. I passed all the psycho-aptitude exams perfectly. I always kept a photo cut-out from a magazine that portrayed two GOI Raiders from COMSUBIN in my wallet. Redundant staff was the officer's response. I tried to fall back to civilian life, trying to help out in Dad's shop but, obviously, I didn't last long.

So, I became a delivery master. I was eighteen with a driving license and a burning desire to drive around the city. It wasn't as fun as I imagined and I soon found myself doing two or three makeshift jobs at once just to make a living. Despite everything, I still had the desire to pursue a military career.

I tried again with the Army and proposed myself as a Fixed Volunteer. They got me right away, but not Special Forces. Alpini and assigned somewhere on the border with Austria and Slovenia. I liked it. I loved the idea that all recruits, regardless of their social background, were the same. It was a sort of democracy imposed from above.

They whipped me into shape there and I learned through recruit training concepts that were previously foreign to me such as discipline and individual and group responsibility. For the first time, I began to enter a group that accepted me for my skills and not because I came from a wealthy family.

I stayed there for four years and I learned to do a little bit of everything. Additionally, I did many joint exercises, even with other NATO armies, where I learned things that would come in handy in the following years. I had finally gotten into some sort of acceptable routine. I had my routine, I had a salary, though it was a shameful one. But at least I had a "social position" that I could show off those few times I returned to the Canaletto. I was out of the neighborhood, but many of my childhood friends were trapped there. Instead, I had made it.

Yet, I needed to do something more in life.

I began to cultivate a new career path: becoming a tactical shooting instructor. Putting all my meager savings together, I went to do some shooting master classes in the United States. My English was pretty bad, but I was a fast learner. When I returned to Italy, I spent my weekends using my salary on ammunition training in various shooting ranges and doing paid seminars. This was my life for a while in the early 2000s.

During this period, I learned they were recruiting civilians to form armed escorts in certain troubled locations throughout the world.

At the time, most of these companies providing these services focused their business in Iraq, which had been devastated by the Second Gulf War. There was a need for civilians with a military background (often presumed, in fact) to stockpile Western-owned assets or installations in Iraq. The pay was substantial and you could only enter if you had the appropriate knowledge of the environment. Then there was another front, which in those years guaranteed a considerable income for a few months of mission: the anti-piracy stocks in the Indian Ocean. Someone recommended me to one of these companies that provided guard service to shipowners and they enlisted me as an anti-piracy operator.

I boarded one of the ships and the methodical manner I had acquired during my military service collided severely with the relative indulgence that dominated in that kind of armed guard business. Except for a few times, I essentially died of boredom for months.

Back in Italy, I was more confused than before. I had accumulated a specific curriculum for handling firearms and teaching their use, but still, I was unable to find a solid job. I had gained awareness and a personal vision of the world and I tried to understand where I could take advantage of my abilities for good. For a higher cause. I got interested in the situation in Iraqi Kurdistan. I was intrigued by the Kurds' resolution to become the weapon to defeat ISIS. They needed help, weapons, logistics, and men. The Kurdish Cause attracted people from all nations and political and religious beliefs every year. These people presented themselves and the Kurds assessed their inclination to fight with them against ISIS.

I didn't reflect on it too much and found myself wandering around a Kurdistan city, armed exclusively with an iPad with my weapons training videos on it, a few thousand euros, and English skills far from perfection. I wanted to propose myself as a military instructor for the Kurdish military. I knocked on all the doors of the Kurdish army and police barracks. Sometimes, they wouldn't open for me. Sometimes, they listened to me for a few minutes, smiling, and then politely pointed to the door. More rarely, they watched the videos on the iPad with interest, but the response was always the same. "Maybe next time. Thanks." Money began to run out, as well as barracks to question. It was through a chance encounter that a Peshmerga officer took a liking to me. I was unofficially recruited, and for weeks my job was only to serve as the orderly of the barracks commander. It was unnerving. I didn't know my function. No one told me where I would end up, but at least I had three meals a day and a roof over my head.

Then, they handed me an M4 carbine one day and asked me if I knew what it was. I showed off my marksman and gunsmith skills. I discovered with horror that I was the only person in the entire barracks who knew how to reset a firearm. Thus, I became the official "optics and rear sight calibrator" of all the barracks in the district. For weeks, I tagged whatever gear the West had given to the Kurds to fight ISIS, from 5.56 NATO carbines to machine guns of every order and grade. Of course, I also got my hands dirty with Soviet-designed weapons and fell in love with the PKM machine gun, which I had never used before.

Time passed and my work was highly appreciated. But I hadn't turned my life

Me nearby the Kirkuk citadel during the celebrations for the independence referendum

upside down to become just any gunsmith. I wanted to see the front line, the action. Fight. My patience and persistence were rewarded and I was chosen to become the instructor of a fledgling special police unit. My adventure had begun.

3

THE AWAKENING

The sun was high in the sky and it was hot. I needed shade. In my backpack, I had another poncho sheet, some paracord, and some aluminum pegs.

I got up and made some adjustments. After a few minutes, I had made an excellent parasol and remained seated in the shade under my makeshift tent. I spent the rest of the morning in an alternating state of sleep and wakefulness. I was hungry, so I opened a couple of cans of tuna. I took care not to leave anything in the field and recover all the waste I had produced. After the meal (if it could even be called that), I tried to rest again. I tossed and turned, but I couldn't sleep for more than twenty minutes in a row. By then, it was 5 p.m. and I was overwhelmed by the urge to turn on the phone to try to figure out what was happening to my men. I fought against the desire all day. I didn't want to risk being spotted. I had my goal and, according to my plans, I could only turn on the phone near Peshraw's uncle's village. I took advantage of the sun to recharge my power banks and various devices with the solar panel. I studied and examined the digital maps and observed the satellite photos of the itinerary. They were recent photos and I considered every detail.

What if I move before sunset? I don't see anyone… there is no movement. Maybe I should do it. But why risk it? The truth was, I wanted to cut and run as soon as possible. Gradually, I began to re-pack my materials and prepare myself for the next march. I enjoyed another spectacular sunset and made myself another coffee. After all, it was still my birthday.

Just before the sun disappeared behind the horizon, I set off. I spent the night marching on more tortuous terrain.

I was able to sleep. I ate and I even made myself two coffees. Also, having consumed some of the supplies of water and food I had in my backpack, it was easier to walk.

Nonetheless, I felt tired. Maybe it was my adrenaline that was dropping and I was paying for the fatigue of the last few days. I had planned to go north quickly, meet the river, and follow it until I reached the bridge directly, where I would meet the uncle. If I went faster, I could catch up with him at a decent time and spend the night near him. Meanwhile, I crossed a busy area because I could see lights in the distance and hear moving vehicles and dogs barking. I quickened my pace. I had to find a safe place to stop and try to contact Peshraw, who would tell his uncle to pick me up under the bridge.

The night passed more or less like the previous one, but I kept a steadier pace. I walked along a branch of the dry river. The bed consisted of stones and more stones, so my feet hurt a little but, I kept moving, gritting my teeth. Throughout my listening breaks, I could perceive more human activity than the day before.

I left at an even faster pace, continuing north until I crossed the river called *al-Zāb al-Asfal*.

After a few hours of brisk walking, I reached the river. The banks were muddy and swampy with thick vegetation that could cover my path.

I went through the procedure for the umpteenth time. Once I was close to the bridge, I would call Peshraw's uncle and send him my position. If Peshraw had been there in person, it would have been easier because, as soldiers, they communicated in MGRS standard and I could have been reached at any agreed point. But in the case of his uncle, how could I have communicated where to pick me up? We had agreed on a point known to the villagers and I didn't want to risk being seen. Since it was a village on the border area, I needed to be careful not to be noticed.

I was a bit afraid to turn on the phone. I figured I'd get some bad news, besides the damn fear of being tracked electronically. I stopped and put my backpack on the ground. My back was in pieces. I put the poncho over my head for the umpteenth time and checked the point on the map. There were only a couple of miles left, going east at the RV point. Finally.

I had to turn on the phone and text Peshraw. What if he didn't answer? What if the uncle wasn't available? What if someone was waiting for me to catch me? What if Peshraw sold me out? I shook my head to get rid of all the doubts and fears. *Come on, Alex. Take heart. You have no alternative.*

I summoned courage and changed the Asiacell SIM card with that of another operator not in my name. I set it to silent mode. Three, two, one… I pushed the power button. I pressed my thumb on the speaker to muffle the damn phone animation that plays when it turns on. I looked at the display. Full battery. After a few seconds, the signal strength bars appeared. I had disconnected the data connection to makc it more difficult to locate the phone. I opted to write a simple SMS in Kurdish:

"Cowni? Basci? Lakwe?"

"How are you? Doing good? Where are you?"

I didn't even have time to reach the messages screen when about twenty text messages arrived suddenly along with countless notifications of missed calls. Peshraw, Aram, Salar, my captain, and some other friends had tried to call me. I also noticed numbers not in the phonebook, which worried me.

I sent my message and switched the phone airplane mode. I waited five minutes and then woke the phone. It was a long five minutes. Maybe four and a half minutes. I had lost track of time. I was perfectly aware that I had just reported my location electronically. Having sent an SMS, the phone had hooked up to a cell tower in the area and any intelligence apparatus that had been on my trail would have my approximate geolocation in the area. I had to get away from that spot as soon as possible. I reactivated the phone.

Answer please. Peshraw... answer... I thought through gritted teeth. The phone vibrated in my hand. It was an unknown number. I denied the call. Who could it be? Maybe Peshraw's uncle? What if something happened to Peshraw? I sent a message to Salar:

```
"Hello, brother. I'm near
the R.V. Where is Peshraw?"
```

A few moments passed.

```
"Soresh! Everything okay
here. Everything okay?
Where are you?
Where is Peshraw?"
```

I answered quickly. My interlocutor let about ten seconds pass before answering me. It was agony waiting for the answer.

It finally came: `"It's coming to you."`

What do they mean, he is coming to me? I thought *How is this possible?* The mystery number sent me another text message. A string of numbers. They were coordinates! The message concluded our Word of Order. A keyword that I do not intend to disclose. It was Peshraw! Or someone from my team. Only we knew the keyword.

I put the coordinates back on my PDA. I pinpointed the position. Around a mile to the east. I understood from the satellite photos that it was the bridge itself. I calculated an hour to reach that point. I wanted to approach slowly, identifying who or what was waiting for me. I replied with the answer keyword and added:

"BASHA, YEK SAHA"

"Well, give me an hour."

My interlocutor replied with a time window. Who was waiting for me? Was "the uncle" able to read and communicate in military code? Could he read coordinates in MGRS format? And how did he know the keyword? There was no way I could verify. I wrote to Salar again. I got no answer. I unplugged the phone, folded the poncho, and put it in my backpack. Then, I walked to the RV point to meet my mysterious new friend. Again, a dialogue broke out in my head: *What if it's a trap? A trap set by whom? There is no way that, with the mess that happened, they come looking for me. Why not? You are still a Westerner in Iraq during a goddamn war... Or did you forget, you idiot?* I had my own way of motivating myself.

I approached, slowing my pace. I was covered in the vegetation that grew along the river. My heart was pounding in my chest. I was at the showdown. I cocked my M4 and the Glock. Anyone with bad intentions would have found me ready. I entered the tactical mode. Eyes and ears wide open. The vegetation cover obscured my progress, but at the same time, reduced my ability to spot a potential problem early. At this stage, hearing and smell were my only tools for interpreting the surrounding environment. I slowed my pace and moved carefully to my feet, first tasting the ground, step by step. I couldn't afford to step on something that made too much noise, like a dry shrub, and I absolutely couldn't slip and lose my balance. I would have made too much noise. So, I walked at a slow, steady pace and tried to anticipate anomalies around me, all while keeping the rifle ready to engage any hostile presence. The weapon was ready, safety was off, and my finger was along with the trigger guard, ready to move on the trigger at any time.

In this phase, the night vision device was necessary. In specific cases, compromises have to be made. Is it better to have a greenish vision, but with a limited field of view and shallow depth of vision, or is it better to have an eye that has become sufficiently accustomed to the darkness and residual night light? I am not saying that night vision goggles are useless, but never forget that a human eye in the open that has become accustomed to the dark still has something to say on the battlefield. A human eye can find small bright details and take advantage of peripheral vision. If you want to shoot accurately at night, you can do it only and exclusively with a night vision device. In my case, I was using an AN/PVS14, a military model of a monocular viewer. One eye saw through the night vision lens while the other was perfectly accustomed to the dark. It takes a lot of training, but this type of visual setup allows you to make the most of both types of eye input. The brain receives visual signals processed differently, but the benefits are enormous once you get used to them.

I got closer until I reached about three hundred meters from the goal. I saw the bridge clearly, but no one nearby. With the night viewer, I saw there were houses near the bridge. Although it was still late at night, some had their lights on and the usual concert of dogs barking. I moved even closer and surveyed the surrounding area. I decided to leave the backpack and continue. In case something had happened, I would be more agile and faster. I marked the backpack with an IR stick and recorded the point with the GPS. To reduce the brightness of the IR sticks, I would wrap them in advance with adhesive tape. The IR sticks were particularly bright when spotted by a night vision device or a drone equipped with the same technology. I always assumed that any pursuer had the same night vision technologies as mine. After a while, I stopped in the middle of the vegetation and reactivated the phone, still covered by the poncho. I had saved my mysterious friend as UFO1 in the address book. I read the message from UFO1:

"Lakwe? Where are you?"

I answered, giving the coordinates of the grid.

```
"Well Soresh, I'm coming now."
```

I stood waiting. I had approached another hundred meters and could see the bridge, the village, and the road clearly.

An off-road vehicle arrived. From a distance, despite the darkness, I recognized the silhouette of a Toyota Land Cruiser, which was a standard model in the area. But I was shocked. It wasn't just any car... It was my service car! *Are you mocking me!?*

I watched. The off-road vehicle arrived with the lights off. The Stoplights did not even come on when the run stopped. The driver's side door opened, and the interior lights did not come on. I had personally disabled the interior light when the doors opened and I had modified the car to turn off all the lights. It was a useful strategy during night driving with viewers. I only saw one person.

Another SMS.

```
Where are you? It's
Peshraw.
```

I approached slowly with the night viewer lowered over my eyes, taking advantage of the vegetation cover. I recognized the short and heavy silhouette of the man. I continued slowly, climbing the ascent of the bridge pillars. I kept walking with the M4, always ready. I finally got a clearer view of the vehicle and its driver. It was Peshraw with my car!

"*Pssst...*" I hissed.

"Soresh!"

He came toward me and hugged me tightly. It was him, and I could hardly believe it.

"Yes, yes... there is no time now. Let's go", he whispered. I ran to retrieve the backpack and loaded it into the car. Peshraw smiled at me and I hugged him again, squeezing him like a puppet.

"Let's get out of here, friend! Yalla! "

"I told you I wouldn't abandon you!"

"I had no doubts, and you also brought me the car!" I had noticed that he had a few more bullet holes than I remembered by heart, but it was okay anyway. I was happy to see that friendly face.

"We will spend the night with my uncle. We cannot go anywhere now. There is fighting between the Peshmerga and the Shia militias here near the border checkpoint. We cannot move."

I did not jump for joy upon hearing that news. I was not thrilled with the idea of staying on the border for any longer, but I trusted Peshraw. His uncle's house was slightly out of the way of the village.

It was a detached house and we parked inside the wall that surrounded it. The lights were out, and everyone seemed to be sleeping.

"Peshraw, tell me what happened. How are the kids? Where are the captain and Mariwan? " My friend's eyes turned glassy, and he looked down.

"Walla Soresh, Kirkuk tawao..." Tawao means "it's over."

"Hezaresheka, tawaoo!"

"Yes, ok, but where are the boys?" I pressed him.

"Some have gone off Dler to the hospital, Soresh. Salar is still at the base. The Shia militias took Kirkuk… They sold us, Soresh. Now they are advancing towards Erbil. " I could not believe it.

"If they advance toward Erbil, it will be a massacre! The Kurds will never leave Erbil!"

"Soresh, the Iraqis will not attack Erbil. They just want to bring back borders as they originally were before ISIS. " I shook my head and asked, "What will you do, Peshraw?"

"I'll stay here with my uncle. My family managed to escape from Kirkuk and I'm here now."

"I am pleased, too," I answered sincerely, but I had too many questions to ask him.

"What will you do? You can't go back to Kirkuk, you know."

"Yes, I know. And where will you go?" I said as I pondered the answer.

"Did you tell anyone in Command you were coming here? I don't trust anyone anymore. "

"Peshraw, nobody knows, only Salar, and you can trust him." He nodded at those words and then I wanted to share my thoughts with my friend.

"If the Shiites try to enter Erbil, there will be a war. And I think my place is there." I had fled from Kirkuk. I was not going to run away from the next fight.

"And how do you think the PDK Peshmerga will treat you? Everyone knows our unit escaped without a fight! And everyone knows who you are!" Peshraw replied worriedly.

"We did not run away! We held that bridge for hours and to evacuate the last civilians from Kirkuk! Who attacked us? Peshraw, think about it!" My fellow soldier looked me in the eyes sadly.

"It doesn't matter now. Think about saving your life. Try to leave this country."

"And how do I leave? Borders are closed! As well as airports! The only way would be to go through Baghdad!"

"And why should you be afraid of passing through Baghdad? What did you do? Iraq should thank you for your service. Don't be afraid, and go home. No one will stop you."

"What if Erbil is attacked? Or Suly?" I replied, full of emotion.

"You are only a man, Soresh. Go home. Spare yourself from this country. Rest now and eat something. For now, it is safe in here, and you don't have to worry." They had made me a makeshift bed with a blanket on it. I lay on top of it and closed my eyes. I fell into a deep and peaceful sleep. I might have dreamed.

My eyes snapped open. I did a quick check: I had the car keys and I had the rifle. But where had Peshraw gone? I got up. It was late morning. There were many people in the village and there seemed to be a lot of excitement. Many families from Kirkuk had taken refuge in that village. I saw Peshraw, who was in the courtyard with his famous uncle.

"*Beani Bash!*" he said and passed me yogurt and tea with freshly baked bread. Not even a civil war stops a good Kurdish breakfast. The food was satisfying and enjoyable. The bad news came soon after.

"Soresh, we have lost the base. Your stuff is probably going to be worn by some Shiites."

"Ah, okay. I also lost everything. Clothes, equipment, personal effects. I have lost everything..." I did nothing to hide my anger.

"There are people who have lost their lives, Soresh." Peshraw scolded me.

"You're right, friend."

I refueled the car and loaded up my equipment. I hid the M4 in the back seat and held the gun in front of me.

"Soresh, there is another checkpoint ahead. My uncle will come with us. He knows these people very well. He will drive. Once we cross the border, he will leave us at his relative's house and you will be free to go wherever you want." He paused. "Where will you go? Suly or Erbil?"

"Not far away, there is a training center outpost where I've worked in the past," I replied quickly. "I'll go there and see if I can lend a hand to the front."

"Go home, Soresh. Show your passport and the Consulate will probably put you on a military plane."

I laughed heartily at those words.

We passed the checkpoint without too many obstacles, and I hugged Peshraw again and thanked him for "saving" me. Without him, I would never have made it.

I headed to the training center. I saw hundreds of Peshmerga military vehicles on the main road, all heading to the border. I got to the driveway and the guards recognized me.

"*Mamosta*! You did it! We knew you would do it! They are evacuating the training center. They're loading guns and ammunition on the pickups. The Shiite militias are coming..."

I reached Azad near the ammunition depot.

"Soresh, what happened? Everyone says your unit left Kirkuk without a fight."

"Yeah, sure. Right… Listen, Azad. I've had some lousy days lately. Can we change the topic please? Can you tell me more about the situation? Anything on the Shiites who are advancing? From where?"

"Here, Soresh. They're coming from here. The order is to evacuate everything and fall back on Erbil. What are you going to do?"

"Well, I'm trying not to get killed," I replied dryly.

"Listen, we need to move this material from the outpost to Erbil. They reported several groups of irregulars. Would you like to join us? We can then make a convoy together and protect each other. "

"Okay, and who's staying here?"

"The guards."

"But what about them? They are only four men!"

"They just have to cover us while we exfiltrate, then they will go back to their village. The Shiites are approaching the border, and no one knows their intentions."

"Okay, I'm down."

I helped load the guns and ammunition. We were carrying valuable and appealing cargo for the armed gangs that roamed the desert. Chaos reigned supreme and shots from AK47s conducted the law. At all costs, I had to try to get to a safe area.

We got on the vehicles. We traveled in convoy along a dirt road for a while and then rejoined with other auto columns. I was calm, I was no longer alone, and I was back in friendly territory.

I left it all behind: Kirkuk, my boys, my unit. Inside, I was desperate. I had lost everything I had fought and battled for in previous years. A multitude of Peshmerga military vehicles was traveling in the opposite direction of us. Everything was falling apart, and I had just gotten out of it. Others were going to fight... in my place. I wanted to be with them. I felt a strong desire to cry, but a warrior never despairs. Never.

Azad looked at me and asked:

"What are you thinking about?"

I was still looking at the military vehicles going in the other direction through the rearview mirror.

"I'm thinking I'm not doing the right thing, Azad. I should be at the front fighting," I replied bitterly.

"You can't overthink certain things, Soresh. You have done a lot for us, for Kirkuk, and for the Kurds. For once, think only about yourself. We'll go to Erbil and decide what to do. But this time, don't get involved." I nodded sadly, but Azad was right. He knew me too well.

After a few days away from everything and everyone, I returned to the central command in Sulimaya. Task Force Black was relocated from Kirkuk and the Baghdad government redesigned Kurdistan's borders. We had lost Kirkuk and over half of the territories conquered during the war against ISIS. After a rest period, I was reassigned to the SWAT unit of the city with a new assignment. The establishment, the education, and the training of a special unit that would work onboard the helicopters supplied to the Military Police. It was the beginning of a new adventure.

Members of Suly's SWAT units pose for a photo in front of one of our MD530 FF helicopters

4

BASHEER

April 2016 - Kirkuk

At that time, my typical day was based on a simple routine. My mornings started with early physical training, followed by maintenance on weapons and vehicles. Afternoons, on the other hand, were more free. Often they were a quiet period with no operations to plan. Nonetheless, I attempted to keep myself busy and to lend a hand to anyone who needed it on the base.

One evening while doing laundry, I felt something different, like an upset atmosphere in the air. Then, I heard yelling and hectic voices. It was common to hear officers shouting from the windows and out of breath from activities, so the shouting did not alarm me. I was too busy scraping the dirt and sweat stains from a combat uniform with a good, old man.

I was doing impromptu hand-laundry with bottled water, a plastic basin, and lots of soap. I wrung vigorously, rinsed, and wrung again. The uniforms looked better washing them this way than in the washing machine!

"Mamosta Shoresh!" I felt urgently called. I dropped my still-soaked clothes and went outside with my soapy hands. I immediately met Captain Kader, his face drawn, nodding vigorously, asking me to join the retinue of noncommissioned officers who were already surrounding him.

We found ourselves in the briefing room, the tension on our faces unmistakable. As always, the captain was busy juggling several telephone conversations at once while taking notes in a small notebook, occasionally nodding and responding with conviction. It didn't take me long to realize that something significant was about to happen. Finally, he put down the phones and declared that Task Force Black had to be urgently activated. I rushed to the vehicle square and jumped into one of the Land Cruisers that formed the column preparing to leave the General Command and headquarters of the PUK quickly. After a few minutes, my doubts found resolution during a second briefing. The situation was straightforward. It was necessary to conquer and clean up the center of Basheer City from ISIS militiamen. A few hours earlier, some enemy positions had already been attacked by the Peshmerga units but now we were asked, as Task Force Black operators, to open a corridor toward the city center to facilitate the entry of a more substantial attack force. It was not a usual request for Task Force Black. We were, formally, a police force. Why did we have to act as an advanced reconnaissance unit instead of regular reconnaissance units? Our unit was not equipped to perform this type of task at our best.

We had no real tank vehicles and had comparatively few operators. And there was a second important issue: my role. Until that day, I had been part of the Task Force Black missions as a Military Advisor. I was armed, sure, but technically just for self defense. My role on paper was that of the "observer."

Now, they were asking me to go to battle on the frontline. It would no longer be a scenario where I would shoot only to defend myself. This situation changed everything. I will be officially going to war without administrative subtleties and without a regular soldier's pay. I didn't even think about it for a second. It had never been a question of salary. I would have followed my men even to hell.

We headed back to our base to prepare the equipment and warn the men. All the Task Force Black operators were urgently needed, even those on a rest period. It was the dead of the night, yet the base was swarming with frenzied activity. All the operators recalled by the licenses showed up on time. Between one cup of chay and another, we began to draw up a checklist of the equipment we would use for the assault. I took care of distributing tables to each operator and driver of vehicles. That way, they could carry out enough checks on all equipment and personal luggage. Then I had to think about the weapons to take from the armory. Based on the urban warfare scenario we would face, I opted for an adequate supply of counter-tank rockets. The RPG was the weaponry of choice in this type of situation, but I also wanted to have AT4 rocket launchers which were light, precise, and sufficiently effective against urban targets. Plus, they could also be used with night-vision goggles. I also asked for dozens and dozens of hand grenades. In combat in built-up areas, grenades play multiple roles. They are perfect for masking a tactical retreat or for breaking close contact with the enemy.

Our NCO was a big, mustached old man named Kaka Yussef. He looked like the Middle Eastern version of Otto Von Bismarck, exuding authority and reverence. He was old school, opting for the strategy of throwing as many grenades as you could. And when he spoke, everyone listened to him.

Before a battle, the checks and inspections were endless. Check of the communication systems, double-check on the batteries, verification of the maintenance status of the vehicles, yet another check of the machine guns on the fifth wheel. Check the ammunition box, ensure the integrity of the shot feed belt, check the basic kinematics of the machine gun. Check and verify, check and verify, check and verify.

After the inspections, we began to load the vehicles with equipment and endowment to deal with any situation. Volatiles to break through walls and halligan tools to break through doors, locks, and windows. We also packed food and sleeping bags to survive at least a week in the field. I was exhausted by the preparations and I still had to face the battle. But we were finally ready. I just needed to know where Task Force Black's sheltered by a pile of sand. I rested with some friends before continuing. The fighting deployment point would be assigned.

I attended the final briefing with all the officers. I was frantically taking notes in my notebook while Captain Kader's brother, Jassem, interpreted for me. Once I received the initial deployment information, I returned to my unit to share them with the foremen. Planning is vital in military operations Clean-cut orders, as well as clear objectives and discussions of any unforeseen events are crucial.

My role at the time was to give information that was consistent and easy to manage. I spoke English and Hoger was my translator. Hoger was excellent at translating even the nuances of my language and men had their gazes fixed on him so they did not miss a word. Hoger had been my interpreter for years at this point and there was a sort of communicative symbiosis between us. While I was doing the briefing, I was looking over my foremen.

Their faces were concentrated, motivated, and showing a clear desire to get involved, to do things at their best. I gave my final recommendations and ordered them to report everything to the members of their respective teams. At that point, I was relatively free and looked around in case anyone needed help. The spirit of the room was high, but I thought it was also important to instill courage and mitigate the tension before the battle, so I went to chat with my Team Delta men to try to gauge their mental states.

They were eager to go into battle. They were good guys, and the thought that soon I could lose one of them in combat tore my soul. On the outside, I behaved like a fellow soldier in the mood for witty jokes. I stared at them one by one. There was Ginger, Heresh's nickname, who was meticulously combing his reddish-blond hair. He was so proud of his hair that he avoided wearing a helmet in battle so as not to ruin it.
"Hair has to breathe," he always said.
Then there was the smallest of the group: Hiwa. He was in the DShK Fitfy cal.. He was meticulous in the care and maintenance of his heavy machine gun, which was why it never got jammed. I was constantly worried about him because he used to be in a highly exposed position on the roof of the vehicle, but he had always turned down any offer of replacement. He felt the role was his responsibility.

Next was Dilshad, called Mafia for his ability to get almost anything by the wayside. He was an experienced gunner who had been assigned a PKM. I saw him devotedly rolling belts of bullets into his backpack. Our vehicle was an armored Hummer and the driver was Mama "Red" Hajar. His hair rivaled that of Ginger, besides the fact that he was a reckless and exceptional driver at the same time. Those skills helped him earn the position of fleet manager and he had become a reference figure for other drivers. He was also a good repairman, which didn't hurt.

Near another vehicle, I saw Camaro. Yes, Camaro, like the American sporty Chevrolet. He owned one painted in a questionable metallic green which sported him impunity on the streets of Kirkuk. To this day, I still wonder where he got it.

Finally, the order came to leave the base. All the men got into their vehicles and the engines came to life in a chaotic din. I was on the head vehicle. I put my arm out the window and twisted my wrist to order them to drive. As we drove away, we entered the streets of Kirkuk and were immediately flanked by civilian cars that accompanied us. Their drivers hoisted the Kurdistan flags out of their windows and laid on their horns as if the home team had just won the world championships. On the side of the road, the crowd cheered us on shouting, "Biji Peshmarga!" We returned their enthusiasm by showing the victory sign with the fingers of our right hands.

When we arrived at the operating arena, the sun had set. We parked the vehicles to form a sort of defensive perimeter while men inside were preparing for the bivouac. The orders were to begin operations just before dawn. I still didn't have all the information I needed and had to get to the Forward Command Post, which I knew was relatively close. I ordered Hoger to find me a vehicle to get there.

He came back a few minutes later in Captain Kader's personal car. I was pretty sure he hadn't asked for permission to pick up that vehicle, but I didn't have time to waste asking questions. I jumped in and we quickly drove toward the Advanced Command Post. Once I reached the building, I asked to meet with General Mariwan. He welcomed me with his usual expansiveness. In the briefing room, he showed me an updated map of the city with the targets to be attacked. I examined the situation for a few moments and judged it difficult, to say the least.

"Sir, are there Western soldiers in the area?" I asked, hoping it was an intelligent question.

"Of course there are the Americans. They are here with us. Go ahead and consult with them, Soresh."

Right before an offensive, we posed for a memorial photo with some operators of the special forces of the Marines MARSOC. Thank you for protecting us from up there.

It was barely dawn when we began the offensive against the urban center of Basheer, one of the inhabited centers with the highest number of Daesh[1] in the area.

During the night, the coalition air force had prepared the field for us with a sufficient number of airstrikes.

The vehicle column began the movement, following the bulldozers that were opening a passage to create a road for armored vehicles because the conventional roads were littered with improvised explosive devices (or IEDs).

The mission of my group was to protect the bulldozers as they progressed, which meant being the first of the entire unit of over a hundred vehicles.

We placed the tanks in the back and the bulldozers in the front while we moved on foot so we had a wider range of vision and a better reaction capacity.

Along the way, we were ambushed by a couple of small groups of terrorists along

---

[1] Arabic acronym for isis.

the way. Mortar shells exploded around our positions and whistled close to our heads. We could not stop, we were the first, and we could only go forward and continue. Stopping would have meant preventing our assault force from continuing. At every kilometer, the bulldozers created strong points by raising embankments, thus allowing us to stop under a solid cover on a human scale.

It was April, the sun was terribly hot, and our unit hadn't shut down for a second. Fatigue was impending.

We advanced by returning fire, trying to protect the bulldozers from the Daesh (NDA) at all costs while they carelessly advanced against our convoy.

They were everywhere. Mortars fell around us. We were surrounded. Despite this, we could count on the Americans' drones. We were able to foresee the attacks and prepare.

The terrorists tried to get as close as possible, taking cover in the tall grass and vegetation, and tried to discourage the use of our air support. It was comforting to receive good coverage from above.

After about a few miles of advancing, it was still for a moment. We took advantage of it to create a cornerstone for tanks.

I approached the bulldozer, intending to get on the mechanical shovel. I wanted to be in an elevated position to expand my view.

"Hey, can I get up so I can take a look?" I said to the driver.

Being there meant exposing myself to fire. The boys looked at me disapprovingly.

"*Mamostà*, be careful not to stay too long!" Salar warned me.

"Sure, just a few seconds," I reassured him.

I signaled to the driver. I was ready.

He smiled at me and lowered the shovel to let me up. I knew I would be exposed, but there was no other way to see beyond the level of the grass. He operated the mechanical shovel and I sat on it. I scanned the horizon, trying to detect danger. I saw nothing but the smoke coming from the bombing of the village.

"Okay, that's enough!" I said. "Let me down now."

I got off the bulldozer and waved goodbye.

The driver wore a large Kevlar helmet in the old PASGT style. He had no bulletproof vest and no other protection. He was thin and short, but he possessed great courage. He always smiled, even though he was in the riskiest position.

I moved away from the position to go behind the tank and regain my cover. At one point, I heard a whistle, followed by a bang.

I was on the ground. The dust kept my eyes from seeing what had happened. Again, that hateful tinnitus in the ears. I crawled behind the tank in search of cover, found the eyes of my soldiers, and turned my attention to the Hummer. I saw the black hood of my armored vehicle covered in broken glass. In that instant, my blood froze.

They hit us, I thought. Everything moved in slow motion. I partially lost my peripheral vision and that damn whistle in my head that tortured me.

I only saw my Hummer. The sapphire-blue glass shone incredibly in the sun. I was so enchanted observing that glitter, all other sounds were muffled. At one point, I heard my boys knock on the glass and tell me to look to my right.

I didn't understand. If my Hummer was intact, where the heck did those fragments on the hood come from? I turned and saw: the boys of the Controcarri squad with their mouths wide open, stuck in a grimace of pain. The rear of the bulldozer was completely on fire. Something had hit them. The village was more than a half mile away. Who could have reached it with such precision? It could only mean one thing. They were close. I tried to recover and immediately activate the device. I didn't make it in time. The shots started whistling at us and my team took cover behind the vehicles.

I fired my weapon in the presumed direction of the anti-tank missile. Hell flared up around us. I remained focused on finding targets to hit with my weapon. I fired a few shots in a semi-automatic succession, not knowing if I had hit my target or not. Then my mind was attracted to something else. I turned my head to the bulldozer.

A few moments passed until I saw him, covered in flames. The driver, burning alive. Time stopped. Things continued to move in slow motion. I watched the flames devour his body and I stood there, helpless.

I could hear his screams. I could feel his pain.

"We have to get it back!" the fighters shouted.

"Stop! Nobody move. I'll go!" I said. "Cover me..."

I left my cover, firing in the direction of the attackers. I jumped. They separated me only a few feet from him. I stopped. I wanted to try to drag him out of the burning cockpit, but the fire had enveloped the cabin. The tank had caught fire.

I was not far from him, but I could not do anything. I saw him burn alive. He was dying before my eyes, and I could not do anything to save him.

I felt helpless. When you find yourself in such a situation, you don't have time to think. To reflect. You can only assess the risks and try to save as many people as possible by avoiding further losses.

This is what I did at the time. I decided not to expose myself to enemy fire and flames in a desperate attempt to save someone who probably wouldn't survive. However, I could not have sent anyone else from my team. They would certainly have tried saving their teammate, putting their lives and that of the rest of the team at risk.

No, I couldn't afford another fallen one. That day I made a choice. I made a decision that, even today, I feel I pay for day and night.

The boys saturated the area with return fire while the tank fired its cannon. I felt the powerful displacement of air created by the shot. I got on the radio.

"We are under contract!" I yelled as I tried to get my head back on track.

"We have seen!" they answered me, without adding anything else.

Some Iraqi helicopters flew low and unleashed all their firepower.

It was chaos.

A few mortar rounds reached my position and I was thrown to the ground again. We activated air support, which rushed to our aid. They used air-to-ground missiles to give us cover.

"Cease-fire!!" I shouted. "All right? Sam, do you hear me?"

Endless moments passed. Then finally, the answer came:

"Hey, Bro. Is everything okay?"

I breathed a sigh of relief.

"Yes, everything is okay. Can you confirm that all the targets have been engaged?"

"Yes. For now, we don't see any movement."

A ghostly silence descended on the

scene. We were all untouched, apart from some injured. Salar had been hit in the head by a splinter. I lay down on the ground, waiting to see something move. We stood there, motionless, thinking of our driver, who had died in the flames a few moments before.

The evening came, and with her, the order to fall back. We had to approach the village from another side, but fatigue was prevalent among us. We were all in pieces. I dug my hole and got into it in search of a sleep that came very late.

What if I got off the bulldozer twenty seconds later? What if I tried to retrieve the driver? Many of those "what ifs" still echo in my head today.

The night passed quickly with a thousand discussions about what had just happened. The scenes passed us by. Where did we go wrong? Could we have somehow predicted that attack? We had done what we could. That was the only thing that mattered.

Despite the reassurances I received continuously about my work, I could not get that scene out of my head. It was me who revealed the exact location of the bulldozer to the attackers. If only I hadn't decided to go on top. If only I hadn't been so big headed. But that was the only way. We couldn't figure out where our opponents were, there was no other way.

"Look, Alex, don't blame yourself for anything. War is like this. I believe you have made the fairest assessment. Imagine if you had been injured. Who would have guided us into the village?" Hoger's voice was comfortable, but that didn't calm me down.

"I don't know, Hoger. Maybe so, maybe not. I haven't the faintest idea!"

We spent the night watching the bombing, which generated large explosions and flashes of light in the night. The jets flew all night, preparing the ground to enter the city. The sounds of the detonating bombs were like distant lamentations. War drums, beaten by giant hands.

We knew the terrorists were staying safe inside their tunnels. We dug holes to sleep in. I tried to rest, but between the explosions, speeches, and thoughts, I slept very little.

"Alex, are you awake?" It was Salar's voice calling me.

"No, I'm sleeping..." I replied.

"Take a rest and don't think about anything. You are a good commander. Don't listen to others. They don't know you and they don't know who you are!" he assured me.

"Thanks, Salar. My friend, I try to do my best..."

"I heard Mariwan. We're going to Basheer tomorrow. Are you okay?"

"Yes, Salar... I'm fine!" I lied.

I looked at any points of strategic interest on the digital map on my tablet. The map was well updated with recent satellite photos. I could even see the buildings destroyed by bombing in the weeks before the attack.

No matter how hard I tried, my strategy would still not be considered by our generals. They wanted us to search the village house by house. Regardless, I marked the points of interest on the digital paper and what our sector should have been with our entry point. I tried to examine all the details and memorize them. I wanted my whole team to have as much information as possible regarding what could happen in the coming hours.

The buildings were small and low. The streets were unpaved and narrow. We touched the entrance on the south side of the town, the EOD team in front of us. We owed our lives to those guys. Our task was to protect them during their work, opening the way for them and defusing the explosive traps scattered inside the city.

The IED is an enemy that kills you before you notice. It represents one of my greatest fears: dying without a fight.

It was not the first time we had lost someone and it was not the first time that we were involved in heavy firefights, yet each new attack and each new loss caused us irreparable psychological damage.

I thought back to the moments of the ambush. Many fighters froze, blocked and unable to do anything, unable to act. One could be well trained, have fired all the shots in the world at the range, and have read all the necessary tactical books. But eventually, when you find yourself in certain situations, your brain acts as a kind of animal. If you are brave, you stay and fight and if you are a coward, you run away!

I'm not saying I've never felt afraid. I certainly have, but the survival instinct always takes over. I knew that if we hadn't fought that evil, others wouldn't have done it either, so fighting for me meant surviving.

All my boys in the platoon did great, while the same could not be said of many others who ran away by throwing themselves to the ground amid the chaos. It is true that, in words everybody feels like lions but the reality is very different.

There were moments where my body seemed to act by instinct, almost automatically, such as when my weapon was faulty. My hand moved on its own, changing the magazine without even thinking about it. At that moment, all the various tactics I'd learned were of no use.

Every gesture was fluid, done without overthinking. If you ever find yourself in this situation, allow me to give you some advice. Try to learn something simple and effective, thinking about the places you'll find yourself operating and, above all, use the standard equipment to train in the "unexpected." Remember one thing: speed is nothing if there is no effectiveness. You can be as fast as you want, but you have to learn to deal with the unexpected. You will also have to take into account the psychophysical effects of combat and stress. There is a possibility, a small or large chance, you will not get out of the attack alive, but you must never get overwhelmed by panic. I mean it.

You are here because you have chosen to be. You have decided to fight and, consequently, you have a different mindset from those who are attacked at home by thieves. You are in that place because you have worked to be there and now you will have to fight to get out of it. It sounds strange, but that's the way it is. You have to feel like a hunter, even if you are in the opposite position. Never forget it. It will help you to maintain a clear mental state that allows you to move and think quickly.

A mental attitude is vital in certain situations. We must train our minds first. Otherwise, it will not be able to command the body properly. You have to look within yourself. You have to think before you act. Don't confuse your mind with a thousand questions. Only ask yourself the right ones.

If you are not motivated enough, your attack will be uncertain. And there is no room for uncertainty in such situations. Always be honest with yourself and loyal to your team. Those are the only things that will bring honor to you and the people who love you.

Basheer. After requesting the air support of the coalition, my team members and I observe the village on fire, behind us the wreckage of the Bulldozer with the driver's lifeless body inside.

5
ATTACK ON KIRKUK

MOSUL - October 2016

Some of the Task Force boys were playing in the river. I don't know where or how, but they had managed to find a soccer ball. It looked a lot like the one I played with as a child. Heavy and half-deflated with black and white diamonds.

To my surprise, the ball had the Italia 90 logo on it. What the hell was an Italia 90 ball doing in the middle of the war in Iraq? I soon discovered that Iraqis had a real passion for sport, so much so that they developed a small amateur team for each unit.

The Task Force Black was no less, even if, unfortunately, we always had to play wearing our mimetic, due to the QRF shifts that involved detachments.

We were in the middle of the war, but the boys did not miss the opportunity to dribble that old ball, kicking away the tension. Some of the soldiers positioned themselves as fans, while others washed their clothes in the streams, trying to hang them on dangling lines between our old and tired Hummers.

The Hummers were left to the Iraqi army by the Americans and later given to the Peshmerga. It was less expensive for the Americans to leave their equipment and vehicles in Iraq than to take them back to the USA once the war was over. So after almost fifteen years of service and fighting, the Hummers were still functioning well. Most of the interiors had been patched several times and the same went for the engines. All the vehicles had armored glass but had been hit in previous attacks which compromised the tightness of the center in the event of other impacts. There were also some bullet holes on the vehicle bodies.

Our logistics section jumped through hoops to allow us to have vehicles that always worked and those guys did their best. I remember a time we were in the middle of a fight and the repairman intervened to reactivate a broken-down vehicle. They were real war machinists!

The offensive in Mosul had started three days prior, amidst the dusty plains that preceded the city. We were tired, dirty, and covered in sand. That river was a real panacea for everyone. The water was running, fairly clean, sweet, plesantly cold, and about half a foot and a half deep. It was possible to sit in it submerged up to the mouth. The banks were soft and made of clay, a real pleasure for bare feet that had been cooked during days of walking. I never thought I'd find myself taking a bath in a river in October. The sun was high and quickly warmed my body, cooled by the water of the river. I found that moment almost surreal, but it was all true. We were just a few miles from the Caliphate and we were underwear bathing in a river in the middle of the decisive offensive for the fate of the war.

The moment was broken by the clear and direct voice of Captain Mohamed. I could have distinguished that sound, firm and resolute, from a whole crowd.

The unit was ordered to rearrange and be ready to receive further instructions.

"Salar," I said, "weren't we supposed to wait for support units before moving forward?"

"I don't know, I don't know anything..." he replied, staring into space with tired and deep eyes.

"You never know anything," I smiled, but Salar was worried.

"Make sure you put your uniform back on and dry yourself off! Let's try to understand something."

Salar was not just a friend. He was my Sergeant of the group, my right hand on the operational level, and was respected by everyone on the field.

I joined the captain. As always, he spoke into his two telephones. I went to Mariwan.

"Well? What do we do?" I asked him.

He motioned for me to wait.

"Waiting? Waiting for what? Let's move forward. Are we going to Mosul?"

"Wait, Soresh!" This time he showed me the palm of his hand.

The Captain nodded and replied almost obsequiously. "Sure, sir. Immediately, sir!"

He found my gaze and nodded at me. I still didn't understand, but I knew the captain very well. Something new and unexpected was happening.

During the offensive, we had met resistance in the villages. They threw several VBIEDs at us and I used almost all of my medical equipment to treat the wounded. I also fired two of my AT4s and, with one of them, I had even hit one of those damned kamikaze vehicles.

We could not continue an offensive without refueling. Combined with the resistance in the villages, I had to use my AK47.

The captain went to his car, looking in the cockpit for a little more peace of mind to manage his phone calls. "Mariwan, can you tell me what's happening?"

"Soresh, Kirkuk! Problems in Kirkuk!"

I still didn't understand. How could ISIS be in Kirkuk?

"ISIS is in Mosul! Do you see it over there? It is there, not in Kirkuk!" I said.

Mariwan knew perfectly well, but he didn't know how to tell me what he had just discovered.

"Look, don't raise your voice. Nobody knows this. We have received information... ISIS is entering Kirkuk!"

"What the hell??" I couldn't contain myself. "But we're in Mosul!"

"Yes, I know, but they're organizing a counterattack on Kirkuk at our house!"

I couldn't believe his words. I kept looking at him in search of a clear answer and eventually, I collapsed.

"Okay, but there is no one left in Kirkuk! We are all here. Us, Group 70, the first special forces brigade. We're all fucking here and Kirkuk is caught!"

"Look, don't get upset now! Maybe

they'll let us in…" Mariwan tried to calm me down, but I had to do something!

"Okay, but when will they attack?"

His answer took me by surprise:

"According to our information, they will attack tomorrow!"

That word reverberated in my mind. *Tomorrow.*

"Now what do we do?"

"Wait until the captain finishes talking to the governor. They want to send us. Let's see what he tells us... "

A few moments passed. The Captain opened the door and called his brother, shouting his name. Jassim came running, approaching him. They were whispering something, but I could not understand any of it.

They approached me. I was used to seeing Mohamed smiling, but that day his face was hard, serious.

"Shoresh, Walla, Miskilla, Soresh... Miskilla." I didn't understand. I looked at him and tried to catch something.

I asked his brother for help. He usually deciphered the captain's intentions to me.

"Alex… let's go back to Kirkuk, but not all together! Are you ready to take the detachment and go back to base?"

I was stunned by the news but tried to stay focused.

"Sure, but first explain to me in detail what is happening!"

Jassim wasted no more time.

"So we got some information... We know that ISIS will attack targets in Kirkuk tonight. We don't know exactly where, but we'll find out soon. You have to go back to the base. I have already called Jussef. You will refuel and you will remain there, ready to receive reports on the goal. Also, Mariwan will come with you. Is that okay?"

My gaze met Mariwan's as a sign of complicity. We smiled at each other.

"Okay, Shoresh. Go ahead!" continued the captain.

I would have gathered the group, boarded the vehicles on the trucks, and rocketed off destination Kirkuk. I wanted to take part in the battle of Mosul, but orders were orders. I should protect

Kirkuk!

We were tired. We hadn't slept for days due to a non-stop offensive that went on for three days.

I ran to Salar and told him to get the group together. We couldn't miss too much information, so we just gave orders.

Salar was an excellent sergeant, respected, and well-liked by everyone. He never had to make his position known. People just listened to him. Without him, I would never have control of my unit. I saw him with the platoon, as usual. Aram, on the other hand, was still splashing in the river and Peshraw was asleep on the roof of the Hummer.

After a few moments, we were all ready.

Aram exclaimed, "Hey! What about Mosul? We were meant to be here for Mosul, right?"

Aram was a tall man, but he had a baby face. He always had something to say about orders but, afterward, he always brought me tea to apologize. I loved him so much.

Once we arrived at the base in Kirkuk,

we thought about food and supplies. Time had stopped again.

I could see my companion's faces. We were ready.

Trailers soon arrived to load the vehicles and we left for Kirkuk.

It was late afternoon when we reached our destination. Jussef was waiting for us at the door with the set of keys to the armories like a mother at the door ready to welcome her children.

He was waiting for us at the base canteen with some food and freshly baked bread.

Before stuffing my stomach, I asked Salar to put everyone in military formation because I needed to talk to them.

"Okay, guys. Have something to eat, use the toilet. In twenty minutes, I will collect weapons and ammunition in front of the base armory. Jussef will be there ready to wait for us!"

Aram's polemic didn't take much to arrive and I complied with his request.

"Let's take thirty minutes. But be

punctual, guys! Oh, I forgot. Charge your radios and refuel the vehicles!"

I went to my quarters. I was dirty and smelly. I was almost tempted to take a shower, but I couldn't. There was no time. I took the ammo out of my closet and refilled the tanks on my AK47. I went to Mariwan to eat something together, but his phone wouldn't stop ringing.

Mariwan was the commanding officer and, at the time, he was responsible for the operation. Information about the terrorists passed through the captain and then reached Mariwan.

"So… any news? Do we know where they will dock?" I tried asking.

Mariwan ate his bread with Kebab while writing the instructions on a piece of paper he received on the phone with the other hand.

He hung up and said only two words.

"Domis Soresh." They would attack Domis.

Domis was a district located south of

the city of Kirkuk. The Kakay inhabited that area. They were a tribe made up of men with big mustaches.

"Domis, okay! But do we know exactly where? Did they mention any buildings?"

"No, Soresh..."

"And what do you suggest, Lieutenant?"

"I know the captain is returning, along with everyone else. We are the first here..."

It wasn't enough for me. I wanted to understand more.

"How reliable is this information?"

"Very reliable, Soresh. They know where they will attack..."

I got up and went to the Kirkuk map and put my finger on it, indicating our position.

"Look, Mariwan. We're here, right? And look where the potential target area is!" I saw the lieutenant approaching. The circumstances were graver than expected.

"Soresh, what is going to happen is huge. They aren't talking about a single attack made by a dozen people. They are talking about attacks in different areas of the city!"

"Hundreds? How?"

"Hundreds, Soresh! They have been preparing the attack for months."

I could not remain helpless. I wanted to write down a plan straight away, even if the lieutenant seemed to have a clear vision of what to do.

"We have been assigned the Domis area and that is where we need to intervene. Okay, then we are toward the north end of Kirkuk, Domis is the south end..."

"Mariwan is far away. If something happens, we have to get there quickly. If, on the other hand, we are already in that place, we could nip the attack in the bud!"

Mariwan looked puzzled but decided he would talk to the captain about it.

I had told my boys to be out in thirty minutes, but forty had passed. Jusseff was outside the armory, trying to keep the boys at bay.

"Hey, hey. What is this mess?! Salar!" I

shouted. "Where is Salar? Amadebe! Aaaattention!" The boys stood at attention while I continued to look for Salar. Finally, he arrived and joined the others.

"So, guys, before picking up your ammunition, bring the vehicles in front of the quarters and make sure you have all the equipment in order. Check it thoroughly."

I went into the armory and signed the register with Jusseff. I usually had a limit of ammunition and armaments that I could draw from the armory but that evening, Jussef, behind his thick mustache, told me that I could take what I needed, without any limit. The situation was pressing!

I signed up to take charge of the ammunition, the bombs, the flash bangs, and the rockets. I had some RPG7s and AT4s at my disposal that I would use myself. I also collected the ammunition for the PKM and .50 caliber.

I began to distribute everything to my platoon and while the boys were busy filling their tanks and their bottles, I double-checked the radios and distributed them to the drivers, the foremen, and the machine gunners.

At one point, I heard Mariwan shout: "Shoooooooresh! Shoooooooresh!"

The boys were ready. I reached Mariwan to report everything, but he didn't seem particularly interested.

"Okay, okay! The captain told Yussef to give you everything. Now listen to me, Soresh! He told me that he has already contacted the Domis police chief. Everyone is waiting for you at the entrance to the neighborhood. Stay with them and if something happens, wait for the order! The captain is returning with the rest of the unit. That's a big deal! You go to Domis and wait in the local police barracks, okay?"

"When, Mariwan?" was all I said.

Now I was ready. I called Salar to update him, then we made the contacts with the police officer and headed toward the platoon.

I had created a kind of room for

lectures and briefings where I could connect my PDA with all the maps and satellite images. I told Salar to gather the boys in that room since I wanted to do a little briefing. We did not know our goal, but it was still necessary to organize everything.

The boys were ready in their combat gear, half-loads and all. They entered the room and sat down on the chairs, making a lot of noise.

Salar and I started our briefing, discussing the current situation. We looked at the equipment checklists, identified the nearest hospital, sent the grids to the team leaders' handhelds, and identified the area that had been given to us with a trace, highlighting some possible targets. It could be anything, such as a government building, a political office, a public place, and so on. We were thinking of military and police targets. The advantage of working with people from Kirkuk was that they knew their city and each had a relative to call who lived in an area of interest.

We had about an hour to examine the data and find possible targets. We identified a few. A government building and some small police bases. Identifying the coordinates and the possible routes to approach our stand-by position was essential. Besides, it turned out that our position could also be a target. It was thanks to satellite photos that we were able to identify the area accurately. Knowing the environment where we were going to operate was crucial. We tried to identify some landmarks such as mosques, water towers, etc.

My phone rang, it was Mariwan.

"Soresh is late! Just go!"

Salar gave the order to board the vehicles. As always, we were the last to get on. We had to keep everything under control.

The drivers had the direction of the target on their PDAs, but Bestun, the driver camp, knew Kirkuk like the back of his hand as an expert taxi driver.

"Salar, do you have the number of the Domis police chief?"

"I do, Soresh. I call him when we are screwing..."

I made the last radio check before leaving the base.

"Jias. Check! Radio. Check."

"Delta yek Basha, Delta du Basha, Delta se Basha, Delta ciuar Basha..."

We were ready.

Once again, the big gate with the black panther swung open. It was customary for the boys to greet the panther at the gate before going out. So I did.

I told Salar to use a steady pace and try to stay compact.

Kirkuk was an incredibly busy city. There was chaos at any time of day, but not that evening. The traffic was less than usual. It was also cooler than usual, so I lowered the armored glass of my Hummer to enjoy the breeze a bit and looked at the digital map on my PDA. Nobody spoke. The silence was almost loud. I told the gunners to sit down and rest as long as they could, so they blocked the fifth wheels and sat on the ammunition boxes. I couldn't sleep because it was a special moment.

The calm before the storm.

Do the briefing, get ready, and get out. The time that separates us from the fight does not follow the rules of our universe. It is a time that, in some ways, encompasses everything. You don't know if you will come back. Maybe that's your last moment, the last moment to give yourself a cigarette, savor the thrill, observe something with different eyes, say what there is to say to yourself. You have a sort of amplification of the perception of the environment, both internally and externally. You regress to your primal mental status. Many perceptions were amplified, others took second place. Those are the moments when you are alone with yourself, free from fear, where you have made your choice, living in a bubble apart from everything else. Now the past no longer matters. Just the present counts, then and now. You are yourself. Alone, free, and without fear. Nothing matters anymore, just the present. It is a mental and psychophysical status. You know you probably have a good chance of not coming back home alive. You are aware of that, but it's okay. You made your choice and you are there in that slow and heavy metal cage that brings you close to a likely honorable death, as a soldier. You wonder how it will be. Will you blow up? Not notice anything? Will you feel pain? What will you say in your last moments? Will it be like in the movies? I don't care. What matters is that it is honorable, that it served something, and that it will be remembered.

It was 9:00 p.m. We reached the selected point to meet the chief of police. We parked the vehicles inside their tiny base. Salar and I went immediately to introduce ourselves to the commander. He seemed anxious.

Many more cops would arrive at the base in their blue shirts and their AK47 slings. There was a constant coming and going.

I asked the commander if he had any ideas or information about movements in the area. If they had been able to intercept suspicious moves, we could have tried to prevent the attacks. He told us that he had called all his men around him, in plain clothes, to try to get as much information as possible. I asked the commander of the civilian vehicles. We would use those to not attract too much attention.

The situation was tight. All the plainclothes patrols were reporting in real-time on every type of movement in the area.

"In case there is something for you, we will let you know..."

"Excuse me," I said, "What do you mean?" I could not understand the reason for that statement.

"You are here only in the event of an attack. All the prevention activities are my responsibility and that of my police unit."

I could not stay silent.

"No, wait, commander. If a group of terrorists has to be intercepted, that is the task of the anti-terrorism units, not the neighborhood police."

"I know, but now we are doing what we can." The Commander's reply shocked me.

"Salar, tell him not to fuck up! They should not get caught up in their egos. The policemen won't do anything. They'll blow everything up! Please tell him!"

"Don't worry, Soresh. I'll talk to him and we'll contact the captain..."

I was worried. I didn't want these four neighborhood cops to accidentally foil our attack. They were not sufficiently trained and certainly could not help but make trouble. Their job was to monitor and identify the terrorists. We would take care of the rest.

The hours passed and I told my boys to rest a bit. Several people gathered in the small police station. Word had begun to spread.

I decided to lay down in search of sleep that hadn't come easily for a week. I did not sleep in a real bed for a long time, not to mention taking a shower. I had the same underwear on however, I had changed my socks.

Finally, the kebab arrived at the base and my boys shared it with the police at the station. I smelled of river water and regretted not taking a good shower when I was still at the base. Regardless of the concept of hygiene, a shower is good for the spirit and the body. From time to time, I kept an eye on the boys. Some slept on the room floor while others were on their phones. I couldn't take my eyes off the map, trying to memorize the neighborhood from the satellite photos on my program.

II wanted me to identify with the minds of terrorists. Put myself in their shoes. What was most strategic to attack?

I thought a city in the dark would be perfect. The local forces were not equipped with night vision goggles, while the ISIS forces were equipped with them (some third-generation PVS 7s and some optics mounted on their M16s). Eventually, that was what we did, too: cut the power to entire neighborhoods before attacking them using night-vision goggles. What if they used that tactic?

I prayed that the other units were somehow defending the power plants and other important hubs.

At around 2:30 or 3:00 in the morning, I heard a great noise in the captain's office. I ran out of the room they had entrusted to us and Salar came to meet me.

"They attacked! Soresh, let's go!"

"Hey. hey… wait! Where do we go? We have no information…" He didn't even let me finish when Mariwan handed me the phone.

"Soresh, ISIS has just attacked the power plant!"

I couldn't believe it. It was happening for real.

"Okay, but let's stay calm. We have a sector to check."

Salar was agitated. He tried to contact Mariwan again, but nothing. I tried to reassure him.

"Salar, listen. Calm down. Go to the boys and tell them to get ready. If they attacked the power plant, they probably have other targets in mind."

I went into the captain's office with Salar. He too was on the phone or rather, on the phones. How Kurds could talk on two phones at the same time remained a mystery.

"Salar, ask him if the patrols saw anything in our sector. The plant attack means something. Maybe they have the city as their next goal!"

What information did we have?

They attacked the plant and killed those who worked there, but it wasn't over.

Salar was continuously receiving updates.

"Wait up! They say there is also a police station under attack!"

It was the night of the 22nd of October in 2016 and the battle for Kirkuk had just begun.

I wanted some coordinates to report the positions of the attacks on the map so that we could understand something. I passed my PDA to Salar who looked at me a little doubtfully.

"Listen, ask them to explain to you where the attacks took place, roughly, okay?"

My phone vibrated again. It was Mariwan.

"Mariwan! What the hell happened?"

"Soresh, I will send you the grids. Keep yourselves ready! They are attacking Kirkuk. All the units are starting up. Beware of civilians, okay?"

"Okay, where is the captain?"

"He's in charge. The others are coming back now... Be careful, Soresh, okay?" At the same time, I noticed Salar trying to reason with the neighborhood police commander, who was busy on his two phones (I swear I saw him with three or four phones at once).

"Salar, stay with the commander… Try to understand which areas they are attacking. I will go down to get the boys to prepare, okay?

"Okay, Soresh."

The boys were ready. They had already put on their clothes and arranged the material. My four Hummers and I were ready, too. We were just waiting for a target, a damned target.

At 3:30 a.m., I saw Salar running down the stairs.

"I'm in a hotel nearby. A couple of blocks away!"

Behind Salar was the captain along with the policemen, who began to turn left and right.

"Salar, tell me they're not going toward the target."

The very idea of seeing them leave without us made my blood boil. I started calling Mariwan, but both the phone and the radio were busy.

I looked for Jassim, the captain's brother, but we were wasting too much time. Cops were hopping aboard pick-ups in a rage, some without body armor or any planning.

"Commander, wait, please! Tell me where the goal is, and we can try to plan something together ..." I wasn't sure whether I had convinced him.

"It's a hotel nearby, the terrorists have secured themselves inside!"

I wanted to get him talking, having more information about it would allow me to plan something.

"Okay, do we know how many terrorists there are? What kind of weapons do they use? "

"No, we just know that they have entered this hotel and are shooting at people! They also heard some explosions ... "

He wanted to go there with his men, but I did not agree at all. They would have found their death!

"Commander, wait! Please! Tell me where the objective is and we can try to plan something together." I wasn't sure whether I had convinced him.

"It's a hotel nearby. The terrorists have secured themselves inside!"

I wanted to get him talking. The more

information I had, the better I would be able to plan.

"Okay, do we know how many terrorists there are? What kinds of weapons do they use?"

"No, we just know they have entered this hotel and are shooting at people! They've also heard some explosions."

He wanted to go there with his men, but I did not agree at all. They would have found quickly their deaths!

"Commander, once we get there, they will kill you all! This is an organized attack. We need to develop a plan. We can work on it together!"

The NCOs were yelling to go so the attacks continued and they could not waste more precious time.

Before the commander left, Salar intervened. We had to play it all out. We couldn't let them go like that.

"Commander. please. You have been our commander for years. You fought with us. *Mamostà* Soresh knows what he's talking about. Listen to him!"

I didn't have any clear ideas, but I tried

to think about the logic of any attack. It was not the first one I saw and by now, I understood their basic strategy. First, they would mess up a little. Then they would wait for the security forces to arrive and when they did, they would start the second attack. It would be the most devastating one.

"They're just waiting for you to go there and target them! Listen, commander, we must first identify the objective. In this case, the hotel. Then, we must isolate the area progressively, creating safety rings. We need to coordinate with the units in the field."

His response was positive.

"Yes, there are some of mine..."

He was starting to listen to me, but I had to think. He was up to us now, and I had to make him understand it in every way.

"Okay, perfect. Tell him not to let anyone get close. We have to seal the area, then the Task Force will attack the target. We must first know if there are hostages or civilians inside the building."

The commander was trembling. He wanted to reach the hotel.

God, that would have been a massacre! He did not seem to listen to my words and he was willing to run there with his four policemen, full of hope with little preparation. We weren't the American Delta Force, sure, but in that case, we had a much better chance of success than they did.

The phone rang. Mariwan finally showed up.

"Soresh! Listen, all hell is breaking loose. Go with the police and see what you can do."

"Mariwan! Can you talk with this guy? He wants to do it his way, but they'll just get killed!"

"Pass it to me. I'll talk to him!"

I ran to the police commander, who kept shouting.

"We are ready, sir, but my commander wants to talk to you for a moment."

I handed him the phone. He had to calm down. He may have been the station chief of that neighborhood, but we were

Task Force Black and when a Task Force Black officer talks to you, you listen to him!

We had no idea what Mariwan said to the commander. We only knew that he suddenly turned into a friendly person.

He handed me the phone back while the cops got ready on their pick-ups, kicking and screaming and making a lot of noise.

"Soresh, can you hear me?"

"Yes, Mariwan, do you have the coordinates?"

"Okay, let them lead the way. I told them to listen to you once you get close to the point stop."

"Okay, Mariwan, thank you! Trust us, we'll take care of it now!"

"Soresh, don't go in alone. The Alpha team is at the base. I'll send you the coordinates for the Rendezvous, okay? As soon as you arrive, stop and give me a report on the situation. And Soresh...be careful!"

I went to the commander with Salar. He was impatient, but I had to talk to him and this time, he would have no choice but to listen to me.

"Look, we have to do things with a minimum amount of strategy. I need you to lead the way until you get to the hotel. We do not have to get under them immediately, but close. From that position, we will leave the vehicles and begin to move on foot to find out what is happening. We do not know if they are also in other buildings or if they have settled only in that one. If we throw ourselves in, we risk falling into their trap!"

Salar gave him a radio to communicate in real-time. Now we were ready, if that could be said.

We left the base. The hotel was a few blocks away. I followed the itinerary from my PDA, examining the details of the area from the satellite photos. There was a kind of road on the west side of the target, and it was all uncovered. Approaching from that position would have been impossible. Terrorists would be barricaded in on the upper floors, no doubt. We needed large-caliber machine guns to get closer. We knew they probably had undermined the entrances.

I had a strategy in mind, but it wasn't a guaranteed success. I just had to try.

"Salar, tell him to bring us over from the opposite side of the road. Toward their Black!"

We often used this procedure. The black side of the building represented the opposite side to the white one, that is, the one facing the main road. We also had the green side, which represented the right side against the white, and the red side, which represented the left side.

"Let's try to stay a couple of roads away. Tell him to turn off the lights and slow down!"

The sounds of gunfire and explosions could be heard from various parts of the city. Tracer lights were glowing in the sky and we were there, ready to receive updates.

"Okay, Soresh. We're almost at point one!" It was time to send the grids to Mariwan.

People were in the streets. Many armed civilians had occupied them, which complicated the situation. How could we distinguish a terrorist from an armed civilian?

We stopped at a distance, the civilians getting closer and closer to our vehicles. The sound of the gunshots did not stop. The neighborhood was literally under siege!

It was chaos. We kept seeing people coming and going, also coming to us. We had to be ready. We couldn't lower our guard.

Suddenly, some of them started screaming, pointing to the hotel with their arms. We had to collect as much information as possible before attempting a counterattack, or it would be the end.

There was the hiss of bullets, a sign that they were firing from above our heads. The urban area was similar to many Italian suburbs. From our position, it was possible to see the upper floors of the hotel. I told the boys to stay in cover behind the vehicles. The shots continued to explode over our heads.

"Machine gunners in position!" I yelled "Three-sixty coverage, okay guys?"

"Ok, *Mamostà*!" they said in unison.

I could see the determination in their eyes. We were ready and had to get in now!

The police chief picked up his, while Salar and I tried to understand what was happening inside the hotel to find the fire. At one point, the police chief started shouting.

"They are over there! Don't you see?"

I definitely saw them, but unfortunately, I was worried more about what my eyes could not see. Where were the other terrorists hiding?

"Soresh, the captain wants to go to the hotel." Salar kept me updated on everything.

"I understand, but did you hear Mariwan? Do we have permission to enter?"

"I sent him the grids, but he hasn't answered me yet..."

He didn't want this. We had to wait.

"Okay, bring the vehicles closer. We'll surround the building. We'll send the armored vehicles forward. We will use them as cover. Inform the gunners. As soon as they receive the order to shoot on the upper floors of the building, okay?"

Salar nodded. He managed to stay calm and follow the orders. This was crucial, especially at a time like this.

"Salar, listen, take those cops and tell them to calm down! They have to stay behind us so they can get cover. It is necessary to remove civilians. Too many people are not involved here!"

I finally managed to get in touch with Mariwan again.

"Mariwan, can you hear me? There is quite a mess here. We are now approaching the building. I am sending you the coordinates for the rendezvous for the Alpha detachment. We are preparing the target from the black side. I will try to isolate the rear sides of the targets, but you have to get there first, okay?"

"Perfect. Send me the coordinates and isolate the area, but don't get in. Wait for the others. Do you copy that?"

"Roger!"

The shooting continued and I had to try to contain the damage by isolating the building. The commander kept telling me to enter, but until I received the order from Mariwan, I could not move.

They were shooting at people in the neighborhood. They would not stop, but we had to wait for help or our efforts would be wasted.

"We must secure the area before getting into the building and avoid the arrival of more civilians before they enter the sights of the terrorists! We will move together to the corners of the hotel, then we will wait for reinforcements and enter."

We got closer and closer, the shots exploding inside my head. My ears whistled. The noise was deafening and the senses began to suffer.

We reached the right corner, some shots hitting the wall not far from us. The shots were not volleys, but they were rhythmic, used with parsimony. It was dark, and there was no electricity in the neighborhood. How did they manage to aim accurately and shoot in the dark?

We tried to spot the flashes of their rifles, but in the chaos, it wasn't that simple.

The men with the .50 caliber machine guns fired on the upper floors, responding to the shots that came from some windows.

Only the tracers were able to illuminate the deep darkness. I lowered my PVS14 monocular night-vision device to my face. Some of the men were equipped with PVS7 or other models. Shots from the .50 crackled on the building facade, digging holes in the concrete walls. We had not even attempted the approach toward the objective as we were already under engagement. The operators covered themselves, some slipping behind the walls that surrounded the hotel. The only way to safety was to enter the building hall and get out of range of their weapons.

It was true, I was told not to enter and to wait for reinforcements, but staying out of sight meant being under the blows of the terrorists. I had no other choice!

I found a strategic point that allowed me to be out of range and I sent a message to Mariwan.

"We are under contract. We will try to secure ourselves inside the building. RV target on the entrance, white side."

I waited a few moments. I wanted an affirmative answer. It had to be affirmative!

"COPY THAT." Now we could enter.

I let the vehicles cover the corners. We had to beat the windows of the building regularly just so we could cross the street. I noticed that some enemy shooters were positioned on a terrace of the building. I crumbled it with the .50 caliber from my Hummer. Now we had control over the two sides. The other two were missing.

Under the protection of the machine guns, we moved quickly under the hotel wall to bypass it and reach the other two sides.

The policemen stayed behind the vehicles, trying to drive away from the people who had flocked to the scene.

It was common for people who lived in Kirkuk to face gunfire. They don't run away. The enemies attacked their city, their country, and their home and it was unacceptable. The people of Kirkuk would rather die than leave everything without a fight.

The terrorists were inside the hotel and were shooting from the windows. They often changed their position, fired shots, changed their position, and fired more shots. They opened fire with full knowledge of the facts. There were many wounded in the square. They were inside, closed and barricaded, but for now, it was vital to check the entrances to prevent them from leaving the building and disappearing. We couldn't allow it. They had to be stopped!

In a single-file line, we walked along the left side, staying well under the sills to avoid being seen and hit. We passed a service door which I signaled with a *Cyalume IR²*. I quickly examined the entrance: it was an emergency door, one that opened with a handle from the inside as an emergency exit.

I was sure that the jihadists had mined the entrances. It seemed closed from the inside, but someone could have used it to escape. I knew that on the other side, there were no alternative ways to enter and that the only entrance left was the main door. I had to leave someone at the door to check everything while the others continued the fighting. I pointed to Aram, the tall guy who was also last in the lineup.

"Check the back and the door. If anyone tries to get out of here, make sure it isn't a fleeing hostage!"

I told Salar that we needed help handling any hostages fleeing that door. We would have to get cover from a couple of cops to help Aram in case anyone stepped out the door.

---

[2] A chemical light source, autonomous and of short duration.

"Ask anyone who escapes from here to put his hands up. If he does not, then shoot him. We don't know if there are any hostages, so we need to test everyone. Handcuff them and take them away from the scene. We should assume that they are all terrorists, all right?"

Salar communicated the orders to Aram and the policemen.

"Aram, let me know what's going on through the radio, okay? Keep me updated, please."

"Okay," he said, nodding.

I left Aram in his position as we began to head toward the corner.

I saw a wide road with some bodies of armed men on the ground. The vehicles had wide-open doors and the glass was broken by bullet holes. It was crystal clear that the first to arrive on the scene had been killed systematically.

From the corner, we had a good enough view to check the main entrance. I asked Aram if everything was okay and for the time, there didn't seem to be any movement.

Now that we dominated the building entrances, it was time to contact him.

"Mariwan, can you hear me?" I said.

"Yes, we're on our way!"

"We have two entrances. One on the red side and one on the white side. We're trying to keep them busy on the black side. There doesn't seem to be any activity on the main one, but we need to seal up the area!" I said without wasting time, because we didn't have any. Every second was precious but, as always, we had to take the time to plan.

Mariwan followed my directions to the letter. Cooperating would help the team reach the target.

"Roger. Shall we approach from white to red?"

"No, negative. We are already here! Try the other side, we'll join the main entrance!"

"Roger that!"

The Alfa Hummers arrived and, as expected, passed right in the middle of the main road, firing their .50 calibers at the upper floors. We were in the middle of the urban center. They could not risk collateral damage. Consequently, we used the .50 only above the third floor, avoiding the lower floors which were engaged with small weapons.

"DELTA this is ALFA, we are approaching."

"Roger. We're in position!"

The Hummers took their position and the men disembarked from the vehicles covered by the machine guns.

I kept my eyes fixed on the entrance. Someone could come out to meet the assault team.

"Mariwan, are you there?"

"Yes, we are. We have reached the right corner. We are in position!"

It was time to ask that question again. Now or never!

"Can we go in now?" I just wanted to hear a "Yes, affirmative," but the answer was not what I hoped for.

"No, Soresh, wait. The captain said to isolate the area and wait. We do not know if they have undermined the building!"

"Mariwan, are you mocking me? We

must enter! If we don't get in now, this is gonna be a bloodbath. We don't know how many there are and, above all, how much ammunition they have available. What are you waiting for? For them to give up on their own?"

"The captain said to wait, Soresh..."

We controlled the sides of the building and the two exit points, but on the upper floors, the terrorists opened fire on the streets, killing their targets selectively. I could no longer stay there and watch the massacre.

I had to do something. I had to push.

"Mariwan... listen... we must enter! Every minute that goes by, they strengthen and kill more and more people! Do you hear them? They don't shoot randomly. We can't see anything, yet their shots are accurate! They are using night optics. If you don't believe me, look at the shots on the cars... They were all shot with extreme precision."

"I don't know, Soresh. The captain said that—"

"I know what the captain said, but if

we delay the break-in, it will be more challenging to get them out of there. Count the corpses that you can see. The number is increasing more and more!" I was shivering. He had to tell me to come in and I wouldn't give up.

"Look, Soresh, I don't know..."

"You must know! You are the commanding officer. Look, I'm coming in with my team! Let's go inside and try to get a better idea of it. Where are Bravo and Charlie? We need people. We can't free a building with a hundred rooms with only twelve men!" I continued resolutely, but Mariwan did not seem to give up.

"Soresh, you are a problem..."

"Am I a problem? Not the terrorists in there... Am I the problem?" At those words, Mariwan decided to let me move. He understood my intentions and he knew he would not be able to hold me back for much longer.

"Okay, Soresh, just go!"

I immediately called Aram to find out if there was any news in his area. The answer was positive. I could proceed.

"Mariwan sends someone to Aram's position. I take him inside... he has the twelve gauge with him..."

"Copy that, Soresh!"

Now it was time to get serious. I asked Salar to check the boys and proceed with the raid.

Before moving forward, I explained to Mariwan what I would do.

As I mentioned, planning was and is always vital.

"Mariwan, I'll call you if I go out. When we go up, make the machine guns stop firing."

I turned to my men and said only one thing.

"Okay guys are you ready? Let's go in now. Stack formation! Peshraw, where is your helmet?"

"Soresh, I left it on the Hummer…"

I glared at him. "If we get out of here alive, I'll deal with you later…" I was furious.

We entered by climbing the stairs of the entrance, each operator pointing his weapon in one direction to "dominate" the space. Climbing the stairs of a building was one of the most complex tactical acts ever in the CQB. Each operator needed to have a clear understanding of their area of expertise, focusing on keeping the vertical portion of the stairwell, or the empty space around which the stairs wind, under control.

We checked the hall first from the outside, gun barrels pointing, holding them slightly under our eyes to have a good scanning ability. Some cartridge cases were on the ground and we detected some blasts on the walls and ceiling. A sign that perhaps the terrorists had opened fire to make the occupants escape. I was wondering why… why were there no shots inside?

We continued gradually, but there were only a few for such a large building. We needed to pay utmost attention when checking the rooms. There was no space for uncertainty. Due the absence of electricity, the elevators did not work.

It was dark, so we used our night-vision goggles. Through the green lens of my PVS-14s, I could see the environment clearly. I did not activate the IR illuminator of the viewer so as not to blind the others in the team. I had an IR laser on my rifle, which I could use to aim my target and fire with average accuracy.

The boys were jittery, like me. There was no one inside on the ground floor. We avoided being heard and checked all the rooms, making sure not to activate any explosive traps. We moved conservatively, slowly. It was not direct action, but we knew for sure that the terrorists were on the upper floors. Despite this, we could not exclude that some of them could have been stationed on the lower floors to defend the group of shooters located on the rooftops.

We went up the stairs, covering each other. We weren't the Delta force, but we had trained hard at CQB, and it was great to see the men apply the same moves we tried every day in training. We went up the stairwell in the darkness, the sound of gunfire in the background.

"We are coming to get you," I thought. "Your minutes are numbered..."

Our formation was compact, with me on the front, Salar behind me, and Peshraw and all the others immediately after.

I wished I had a ballistic shield, like the ones they use in Switzerland, super light. Unfortunately, I could only daydream about such a thing. My equipment lacked one. The only protection I had available were the plates of my plate carrier and my helmet. But, most importantly, I had my rifle.

"Mariwan, we're on our way up," I said through the microphone.

"Okay, roger. Proceed!"

We went up floor by floor, checking the corridors and opening the rooms silently. It was evident that perhaps the terrorists had let the hotel occupants escape. There were no bloodstains or corpses.

In the darkness that surrounded us undeterred, I whispered orders. We used visual cues and touched each other to manage the action. We didn't want to be found. As we went up, the tension grew, but we knew one thing: There shouldn't be many of them.

"We haven't seen terrorists guarding the stairs..." I thought to myself. Logic told me that they had probably undermined the entrance to the fifth floor, the one the fire came from.

The corridor had some parallel rooms which were closed. We could have torn down the doors and reconnoitered the various rooms, but we would risk making too much noise and revealing our position. It was too risky a move, so we opted to continue upstairs.

As we went up, the smoke and dust got thicker and thicker. We had identified the group's position, but could not exclude the presence of other people. As a result, the deployment moved to always have an operator cover the backs. It was extremely difficult to catch the noises and possible movements of the terrorists because of the continuous gunshots ripping through the air.

Once I reached the landing that divided the fourth and fifth floors, I saw a shadow on the stairs and opened fire.

A moment passed. The figure moved to fire a couple of shots in our direction. Quite inaccurately, thank God.

Two bullets whistled so close that I could feel them on my face and crashed to the ground near the feet of my colleague, who was covering my shoulders.

We returned the fire saturating the narrow portion of space. The two men in front of the formation and I fired about three or four shots each, without stopping, continuing to advance shoulder to shoulder with our legs slightly flexed to lower our center of gravity. With weapons thrown forward, my boys fired a few inches from my head, but I trusted them. I could feel the wave of pressure on my face from the barrels of their weapons, the shells thrown away, and the gun smoke. We were compact, in formation like a Roman phalanx.

At this point, we could also break the silence.

"Go! Go! Let's go on…" I ordered my formation.

I was convinced that I had hit the terrorist, but he had not been neutralized. A shadow ran up the stairs screaming and shooting down in an agitated and imprecise way. "We're the ones frightening you now," I thought.

"We hit him! He can't go upstairs, guys, or he will tell the others..."

I didn't even have time to finish the sentence. Too late. We heard a cry say, "ALLAH AKBAR!" followed by more screams, and then it was chaos. A burst, followed by silence. A crash, followed by a flash of light. The floor vibrated. Dust everywhere. The upper floor that we were frantically about to reach had just blown up.

I remember the smoke and that damn ringing in my ears. I inhaled a massive dose of gunpowder mixed with smoke.

"Soresh! Are you okay? There was an explosion. What happened?"

"All right," I replied, coughing.

"They blew up, Soresh!" Salar whispered, still stunned by the explosion.

"Guys, gather around. We must all go up together now!"

"Okay, Soresh! Back is free…" He indicated Aram with his hand.

"Soresh, they killed themselves! Died!" Peshraw reiterated as he tried to get up off the ground.

"We have to go up and check!"

"Soresh, they're not shooting anymore. I think it's better to wait for the others..."

They were right this time. I should have listened to my team.

"Okay, guys. Keep an eye on the stairs. We'll stop here and wait for the reinforcement team."

I went down a few floors with Aram to have protection in case of a new attack.

"Mariwan, are you there?"

"Yes, are you all okay?"

"Everything is okay. They got blown up..."

"Shhh! Quiet guys. Don't talk!"

The atmosphere became ghostly. The

bursts of shots and gusts echoed in the background. The shots in the distance made an unusual noise. A different, strange sound. The same one that I still hear every New Year's Eve. Here, the soundtrack of war seems to be just that: a soundtrack, but without music, sparkling wine, or friends. Only with barrels.

The radio crackled again.

"Soresh, update me..." I pressed the button on my PTT and put it on standby.

Mariwan would have to wait a few moments.

The terrorists had taken refuge on the top floor, where they could have covered the entire surrounding area at 360 degrees. We had hit the guard and, perhaps, once compromised, they had decided to blow themselves up. What if we had killed him right away? He certainly couldn't have warned the others. What if the terrorists' purpose was to attract us to the top floor and then blow themselves up?

"Enough, Alex. Too many ifs. Now pick yourself up and answer that damn radio."

"I'm here, Mariwan! We have control of the floor and the stairs. We are waiting for the reinforcement team!"

"Mariwan from Delta. Floor five free. I await a reinforcement Alfa team..."

"Mariwan, do you see anything from outside?"

"Negative, but they aren't shooting anymore! No activity detected after the explosion..."

"Roger. Alfa team coming!"

I turned to the boys, wondering if they had heard anything.

"No, Alex. Nobody is moving. All dead!"

"Okay, guys. Let's wait for the Alfa team and then let's go upstairs, okay?"

I told Aram to leave the light sticks on the stairs. We couldn't see anything. The space around me was nothing but smoke and dust, but I didn't want to miss the opportunity to find data. Everything could be useful for finding information. Telephones, documents, any material available were of extreme importance for Intelligence.

The Alfa team marked its arrival with other light sticks.

"Soresh, we're going up the stairs. It's us, don't open fire!"

"Roger, Mariwan. Go on up!"

Finally, I saw them. Or rather, I felt their presence.

"Tell me what the hell happened?"

I started all over again to explain step by step, section by section, word by word.

"Someone must have activated an explosive device..."

"Did you shoot him?" I thought he was joking.

"No, Mariwan, we offered him a coffee! Of course, we shot him. Unfortunately, he had time to warn the others. You know the rest..."

"Okay, has anyone come up to see?"

We were waiting for them to proceed. That was the plan.

"But Shoresh... it would have been better to take them alive..."

At that answer, I could not stop my irony. Holy shit, we had just risked ending up with our Maker!

"Yes, you are right. Next time, we will tell them not to get blown up and to kindly get handcuffed so that we can question them."

Mariwan sensed my sarcasm, but he ignored it.

"You did a good job guys. All the hell happened outside," he added. "Five dead and others injured. Kirkuk is under attack. It looks like the end of the world out there..."

I replied that I was sorry, we had done everything possible, but we certainly could not prevent an explosion.

"Now, let's go up and see. You stay here, too."

The Alpha team climbed and soon found themselves in front of the bodies of terrorists, torn to pieces by the bomb. They also found a large number of weapons and ammunition.

The other two, Team Bravo and Charlie, also arrived and together with the Breachers, they opened and cleared the rest of the rooms. They even found a hotel attendant who was still alive and had taken refuge inside one of the rooms during the attack.

We, on the other hand, went up to the roof. The bodies of the terrorists were in pieces. I saw various parts of the bodies scattered here and there on the terrace.

It was time to go out. We let the guys from the other teams work. A few moments later, I looked up and saw the dawn. In a short time, I saw the officers reach the building. They photographed everything that was left.

The terrorists were armed with some M16s with night-sights, which explained why they were able to engage targets at significant distances in the night.

Once we left the building, we sat in the Hummers. We were exhausted, but I tried to reorganize my group. That night, the shots had cost the sky over Kirkuk. I took off the helmet, my damned helmet.

I could not bear it because it hurt badly. It was not a real Ops-Core. I could not afford one. It was an old ACH that I had found at the Kirkuk market, modified without putting much effort. The harness was not original, but I could not have expected it better at that time. I was trying to make the best use of what I had at my disposal.

I got a terrible headache and threw down a couple of Panadol tablets.

The men were, as always, on the phone.

"Salar, tell them to rest and maintain the position. Soon, we'll return to the base." At least that's what I thought! I saw Mariwan reach me in a hurry.

"Alex! Alex!"

Why did he call me Alex and not Soresh, as he usually did? That wasn't good news. Usually when he used my real name, it meant only one thing: trouble ahead!

"Tell me Mariwan... can we come back now?"

His gaze hardened. As expected, he was bringing bad news.

"Listen Alex, the captain called me... we have another target!"

"Mariwan, we have been awake for days without food and without water! The boys are tired! Are there no other units to send?"

"No, Kirkuk is under attack. Daesh is attacking targets throughout the city."

"Okay, I understand, but where are all the others? Police? Swat? The other counter-terrorism units?"

"They are all committed to their respective targets. They have theirs, we have ours."

I understood. I could not have insisted too much. It was our turn again.

"Okay, what is the goal now?"

Mariwan gave me his pad. I started writing the new coordinates of the target.

"Found it?"

"Yes, I see it. It looks like a government building or something. It's not very far from here."

"No, Alex, it's a school..."

"A school?" I was shaken.

"Yes, a school. There are already units headed there. They will give us support."

He was interrupted by the police chief. He was trembling and wanted to leave immediately to reach the target.

Oh, my God. Here we go again, I

thought. However, I could not say anything to him, given the night I spent in that slaughterhouse, so I thanked him.

"Great job, commander!"

"Thanks for your help," he replied, before remembering for the umpteenth time that we had to move.

"They are in a school. They saw them enter..."

I didn't wait a second longer. We had to hurry. We had no other choice.

"Salaaar!" I shouted.

"Yes, *Mamostà*!"

"Look, we have a new target"

He nodded to me. He already knew everything.

The sun was about to rise again and the sky was beginning to lighten. The night gave way to the new day. The darkness became light. My eyelids got heavier and heavier and fatigue was starting to take its toll.

When adrenaline drops, the body becomes heavy. It was a hot day and I smelled awful. I couldn't manage to change. We had to jump into the Hummers right away and follow the police pickup.

"Salar, can you hear me? Tell the commander that it is no longer night, so we'd better set the rendezvous area away from the target. I'll send you the coordinates, but please tell him, okay?"

"Sure. Roger!"

From the satellite images, we identified the designated area because the photos had been newly updated. Thanks to a gift from some "friends," I had the latest generation of cartography software, which allowed me to draw on constantly updated images. Having the ability to view the pitch from above was a huge advantage to planning.

Along the way, I identified several points of interest. On my tablet, I observed the details surrounding the building. The information I had indicated a possible assault by the armed group.

I didn't know which forces were in the area, but I could hear shots and bangs all along the way. Kirkuk has always had the same problem: women and children were ready to take the field. Civilians would have made it much more complicated, considered that distinguishing a simple armed citizen from a terrorist was not that simple. Trust me. Sometimes we happened to see some elderly people, ready to observe or give advice to the security forces, a bit like our old Westerners do when they stand in front of construction sites to patrol the works in progress.

We arrived on the main road. The armed civilians began waving to be seen. Some shots originated from the buildings behind the road. I headed to that place together with the police chief and some neighborhood elders armed with their cartridges.

"They are over there, in the elementary school. They locked themselves inside with chains and won't let anyone come close… they keep shooting."

"Okay," I replied promptly. "First we have to seal the area, then we'll start thinking about moving toward the target."

As usual, chaos broke out. Everyone wanted to run toward the target without any apparent planning. Here we go again, I thought as I tried to contact Mariwan.

"Mariwan, can you hear me?"

"Yes, loud and clear. Have you found the school?"

"Yes, I feel the situation here is worse than that of the hotel. We need help!"

"We are coming. In the meantime, move toward the sides of the building."

The plan was as follows: we would "take control" over the corners of the building so we could focus on the upper floors and force the entrances.

We approached the building from behind with two armored Hummers, while the other two Hummers would approach once we engaged the occupants on the black side, the rear.

People were on the street, as expected. Once again, distinguishing civilians from terrorists put us under pressure. We entered a small street that overlooked the main road exposed toward the school rear parking lot. From there, we would have had to reach the rear left corner. We would have been exposed to fire until the second Hummer could have rushed behind us to acquire the right rear corner.

Once we got out of the vehicle, covered by the latter, we set two lines which went at a brisk pace. Inside the vehicles, only the machine gunners and drivers would remain.

I wanted the riflemen on the ground so that I could observe better. They would also be quicker to engage.

"Salar, you go with half two. Reach the right corner. We will take the left one. Do you copy that?"

"Roger that!"

"Okay, ready?"

Salar relayed the message to the drivers. They would manage the fire between them and the machine gunners. We should have saturated the upper part of the building to reach the wall and be out of range of their weapons.

We got closer and closer to the

opening. At a certain point, we stopped to cover the movement of the rear Hummer moving to the right. At that precise moment, some shots hit our vehicles and bounced off the sheet metal. On our left, about fifty meters away, we found the corner, but we had to expose the vehicle just enough to be able to use the turret with the .50. During the move, a large amount of response fire from their PKMs reached us, while some RPGs exploded around our position. To return fire effectively and accurately, the vehicle had to stop. We were in the highly populated urban territory and could not risk scattering .50 caliber rounds randomly throughout the neighborhood. This choice would have exposed us to fire, but we also had to direct the fire of our machine guns with the utmost precision.

The vehicle traveled a few meters at a walking pace and stopped to allow the shooter on the machine gun to fire his mighty weapon.

I assumed the kneeling position and

sought cover behind the wheel. From that position, I could clearly see the building and had a good view of the other team, which was still a long way from the right corner.

Once the support team reached its potion, we could move towards cover. The support team had more distance to cross, so we slowed down and increased our fire pace.

We were fighting in the middle of a city with civilians running from all sides inside, often crossing our fire lines. We aimed at the windows, but it was hard to see them from the inside, as they had reinforced the window frames with sandbags. They were well entrenched, in short.

Their fire pace was constant and well organized. I could clearly see the bullets' impact on the sand around me.

"Salar, are you there?" I shouted over the radio.

"Negative, Soresh ..."

"Pick up the pace! We are under heavy fire ... "

"Roger!"

The driver got shot in the thigh. It had probably entered the cockpit passing through the seal.

He was bleeding and yelling. The boys immediately dabbed the wound, but that was not enough. He had to be taken to the hospital right away.

I was equipped with my modified AK47. I had mounted my Aimpoint and its Magnifier on it and, while crouching on my knees, I barely exposed myself to look through my optics. Shots kept bouncing close, but I had to see where they were firing from. They were very cautious about exposing the muzzles of the weapons to do not create flashes that could have shown their positions.

It was day, and the sun was now high, but a muzzle flash was still visible even with that brightness. I leaned over and felt a couple of shots hit the sand a few meters away from me.

From our position, we were able to see the entire rear facade of the building, which was divided respectively into two other sections. We divided the skills of our sectors to engage the whole building simultaneously.

I returned the fire by discharging two shots into each window, five in total, and alternating with the others on the team. The goal was not to hit them but to saturate the area to make them lower their head and not allow them to engage us with precision. This would have given us some time to approach the entrances and break-in. In these cases, we speak of "approach" and it is one of the most delicate and complicated phases of the mission.

I exposed myself from the outline of the Hummer tire, which was my cover, a couple more times to be able to see. Some shots hit the vehicle, I felt them close. Very close. Violent impacts like stones on sheet metal. "Yes, yes, these are certainly for me," I thought.

I returned the fire and hurled another series of shots, this time, slowly and rhythmically, regardless of my exposure out of cover. There was nothing else to do. If I had wanted to fire them back, I would have had to expose myself. I was ready. I looked out again, but this time I had a weapon malfunction. Even the AKs get stuck, unfortunately. I returned to my cover and tried to repair it. By now, I was in automatic mode, I had done that movement thousands of times, and it took me a few seconds to restore the functioning of my rifle. I got out of the cover again, and all of a sudden, I heard a hiss near my chest. A bullet reached the ground behind my Hummer, passing just a few centimeters from my body.

I did not give up. I continued to go in and out of my cover, returning the fire. At one point, I shifted my attention down to the corners of the building. The shots came from there. I could see him, he was moving every time he shot. He was exposing himself too. Drawing the fire on the right side and responding on the left.

I had to think, find a strategy. I didn't have much time.

"Dler, come over me, there is a target

on the right side of the building about one hundred and twenty meters away ... cover me! I have to expose myself! "

"Ok!"

I knew it would respond from the opposite side, so I got into position, resting the front of my AK on the Hummer's bumper, to get more stability. The right knee was raised to provide support for the elbow and stabilize the weapon even more. I would have waited for him on his hypothetical exit point. One-shot would have been enough for me.

The hypothetical distance was about one hundred and twenty meters from my position. I could not be wrong. If he had noticed that his position had been identified, he would have immediately changed it, and we would have lost him.

I had my Aimpoint calibrated at twenty-five meters for close combat.

My Magnifier gave me the ability to see with 3X magnification, plus I could align the red laser on my aiming point.

I waited, aiming for that corner. I was

exposed because to seek more stability, I had to lean on the vehicle's bumper, this would have given me more accuracy in shooting, but it exposed me more to enemy fire.

"Dler, are you in position?"

"I am!"

Dler kept eye contact with Salar. When the boys fired, it meant that the target would be out shortly thereafter. His job was to cover me, as I would have to expose myself to make the shot.

"They're engaging us. Here they are!"

Time stopped, I isolated myself from the surrounding environment. Suddenly there was nothing left, apart from me, Dler, and that one shot I had at my disposal.

I stared at that corner that became my world. I first saw the barrel of his AK with a one hundred-round drum magazine of the big ones, I believe. He turned around the corner, sure that he could expose himself again to shoot us. Time had stopped again.

I had done it thousands of times

during training. I had fired thousands of shots from every imaginable distance, from every conceivable position. I was in a comfortable position, I had stability, and with the heel of my right foot, I could make some adjustments. My target was there, with the body partially exposed from the corner, I should have aimed to the belt, but she was not exposed. I only saw the chest and the head. I could not distinguish any details. It was just a shadow.

I placed the red dot on my chest, pulled the trigger of my AK47 progressively. I held my breath and fired with empty lungs. Dler fired over my head, and some shots whistled on our positions.

He died as if the ground had sucked him into itself. I didn't see the impact because once I pulled the trigger, I lost alignment with the lens, but I saw him falling. I kept my eyes on that corner, he was on the ground. I scanned the area to see if other militiamen would approach him, in that case, I would have been ready.

Nobody came near. Nobody responded to that blow.

"Target shot down!" now we could move on.

I got up, gave the order to my Driver to proceed. I put the safety on my AK, no one answered on the other side. A shot, well placed under the eye, "how lucky", I thought.

After a few seconds of silence on the other side, the fire reopened against us. We were close to being in line with the corner of a house. I took courage, and I sprinted. I had to reach him.

Dler followed me, in a moment, we arrived at the corner. I got down on my knees and returned the fire, Dler did the same.

We had placed our Hummer with the machine gun on the rear left corner, about a hundred meters away from the school, so that we could cover and, in case, beat the two sides of the building. Now we could reach the right side, passing through the streets of the neighborhood, covering ourselves between the houses. Team Two would do the same, and we would be reunited under the wall out of the reach of their weapons.

We reorganized the group. We had cops and people from the neighborhood. We had to divide: the first group had to move while the other would have covered it. I took a look at my PDA map, fortunately, it was up to date, I could see the neighborhood streets.

"Mariwan, can you hear me?"

"Roger, wait for the others, do not enter!"

"Okay, listen, I put two Hummers in position: rear left and right, 100 meters from the target. I advance until I reach the back wall and put the other two ok? "

"Ok, but don't enter !!"

"Roger! Listen, are there others on the other side? "

"I don't know, be careful not to get shot ..."

I showed the point to the boys from my PDA so that everyone knew where we were going. We started moving between the houses, covering each other. Terrorists could be anywhere in that chaos, many civilians were leaning on the doors of the house.

"Stay home!" we shouted, "stay away from the windows."

The armed civilian men remained standing in front of their doors in case some militiamen attacked them.

"Salar, can you hear me? We start moving to reach the RV point. Coordinate the fire ok? "

"Roger!"

We came out right on the street that overlooked the right corner of the building. Some police vehicles from another SWAT unit were present but kept their distance. This was another serious problem. The fact that the different units did not coordinate with each other created a great deal of chaos. Everyone acted according to their logic, and often it was not logic.

I waved, and the agents recognized us,

replied confirming, and told us to move forward, pointing their weapons at the building.

"Hey, did you shoot the one in the corner?"

"Yes, we caught it ..." Dler answered.

"Nice Shot! You hit him in the face ... he kept us all at a distance ... "

"Good Soresh!! Good Mamosta…" Aram said.

There was no time for compliments, we could think about them later.

"Are you covering us now?"

"Yes, yes, go now, we will come too ..."

We walked under the wall, in line with the body of the militiaman I had taken in the face. We ran over, some policemen followed us.

"Stop boys!! Don't touch anything. " I turned to my men.

The policemen poured over the body, removing their weapons and leaving the jacket with some magazines inside.

"He's got an explosive belt! Stay away and let us do it ... "

One of the policemen, the bravest or

the craziest, unbuckled the belt activated by grenade fuses.

"All right, guys," he said as he showed the belt.

He hadn't had time to blow himself up, thank God.

I went closer, I saw his red beard and a minute hole under the eye. I forgot if it was the right or the left, but it doesn't matter now. I can only tell you that he was dead, and he was ugly as the devil. Dirty with a long beard and a blackened face, his long, greasy hair stuck together.

"Well done ..." someone from my team said.

After a few moments, however, I noticed that he not only had that blow but he was riddled with blows. His legs were broken, and he was full of blood, later congealed in his beard. Had they shot him before me? Or had they shot him once he fell to the ground? It didn't matter anymore now, the only important thing is that he wouldn't hurt anyone anymore.

Many of you may be wondering: what

is it like to kill someone? During my training, I have often referred to the concept of the sheepdog, the sheep, and the wolves. The sheep represent that category of people who think about themselves, rejecting any kind of violence. Wolves, on the other hand, are those people who try to harm others to gain personal advantage. Lastly, there are shepherd dogs. They feel an unstoppable desire to protect others. The shepherd dog's appearance, however, is much more similar to that of the wolf rather than that of the sheep, which is why the shepherd dog will never really be "inside" that same flock he seeks at all costs to protect. The mission of the one who has decided to serve the flock is to preserve anyone's life, without distinction, and no matter whether it is sheep or wolves, taking life must always and only be the last choice. None of us want to play God, but there are times when a choice has to be made. In the stages of training, we tend to make the targets resemble more and more the body of a human being.

Unlike the wolf, the shepherd dog must control its strength and place it in a few and determined moments to render the antagonist inoffensive. I would define it as "*applied violence*". A switch one can turn on and off when is needed. At least, this is how society would like us to be, like puppies that, in case of need, are ready to tear the enemy to pieces.

The moment you find yourself face to face with the enemy, you don't have much time left to reason or reflect. He has his Jihad, his mission, and for that, he is doomed to death, while I have my creed, my flag, and the duty to defend innocents. I've always valued life a lot, but sometimes, to protect someone, you have to hurt someone else.

At that moment, I felt no pain, that was not a man, he was a foreigner who had traveled to fight his *Jihad*, a Foreign Fighters, a terrorist, a torturer, a rapist, a killer, a madman, a threat to humans who had entered a school and was deliberately killing women and children. He was a wolf, a cruel son of a bitch, and I did the right thing. It was not the first time, and it will not be the last in the course of the war. I do not regret anything, and I do not look away when I cross myself in the mirror. I did the right thing, and if the world is missing the appeal of some criminal, I can only be proud of it.

The team was compact again, and we could continue following the wall on the left corner; with us came a Hummer that we should have "moved" to the front right corner to have all four corners under control. The machine gun covered the upper floor and was ready to fire in the event of an attack. We had decided to gather the units at the main entrance and force it with the Hummers that were supposed to break through the gate.

Now they were surrounded. We had .50 calibers on all four sides and controlled the entrances. They were stuck inside.

The other units advanced and gathered to cover some blocks of flats in front of the main calculation of the school. From the windows on the side of the main entrance, terrorists shot anyone who tried to get close.

We returned fire and advanced to try to reach the entrance. Forcing it and entering was not that easy. The area in front of the entrance was open and without any cover. We managed to reach a shack located about fifty meters from the entrance. We gathered.

The bullets whistled in our direction but we had to cross that space to reach the entrance and, thus, get out of their weapons range.

"Ok guys, now we have to get to the entrance ..."

I took my position. I counted the boys around me. We had to travel that space without any cover, if not with the fire of our colleagues. I remained in position, observing the entrance to fight. "Guys, we're covered here."

"Shhhhhh, gee, this came close!" I said looking at the cameraman. By now, I was not getting too upset, I was used to the sounds and colors of the battle.

"Ready? At my signal, two will fire, and

two others will shot ... "

"Now! Fireeee! "

I ran, again as if I had the devil behind me, covered by the fire of my colleagues, the hisses were close, but I only thought about running. I reached the wall and we were all together again, compact, with the members of the other team.

"Mariwan ... are we there?"

"Yes, Soresh!"

We brought the tongs to easily cut the chain that closed the gate from the inside. A few shots reached the opening, and a policeman got wounded in the leg. He fell to the ground, and we dragged him behind the wall. Once under cover of my colleagues, I began the first aid maneuvers. It was not a deep wound, but it needed to be immediately buffered, and the injured person evacuated. That was one of those dark moments when you see the blood flow from their wounds and people screaming madly, in that precise moment you remind yourself that everything is real, it was not a movie, you were not there for fun, it was all real.

I answered the fire on the windows. Together with my mates, we crossed the school square until we entered the corridors. They could be anywhere, but we sensed that they had barricaded themselves on the upper floors. We entered the corridor and approached the stairs to go upstairs. I got down on my knees, the few windows overlooking the external courtyard exposed us to the upper floors, we exchanged fire, and then I decided to try to climb up. I went to the stairs, reached the corner, and began to exit slowly. I was locked in my position and tried to keep my left elbow attached to my body as much as I could. I felt the impetus of the action.

He was there a few meters from me, kneeling on the landing. He was just waiting for my head to come out to shoot at me. It seemed like a race to see who would be exposed first. I had to get the weapon and the eye out of the corner contemporary to shoot as the target was within range. I was on the edge of the corner and the terrorist on the other side who was waiting for me to make a hole in my head, behind my teammates. I wanted to get to the point of exposing myself to cover my colleague in the throw of the grenade that would have "cleaned the stairs". I moved with my whole body while remaining pointing, moving my leg inch by inch. A few shots hit the wall, creating a projection of fragments that reached straight into my face. I fired too, maybe four or five shots, my fellow threw the grenade that reached the landing exploding.

We backed away to avoid being hit by the chippings, and Baaaaam, the bomb thundered inside the building.

I turned around and said:

"Hey, this was the powerful one!"

Silence.

"Allah Akbar, Allah Akbar!" the terrorist shouted victoriously from upstairs. We hadn't taken him or killed him, and he was yelling his battle cry, inviting us to go and get him.

We tried several times to climb the stairs, but without success. There were two entrances to the upper floors, but it was unmanageable to lean out of corners and climb up. They were extremely organized and coordinated in managing the fire. Terrorists fired in bursts down the stairs, throwing hand grenades that exploded downstairs. We were injured. Shrapnel of grenade took me straight in the thigh, I did not realize it instantly, but a few moments later, it started to burn. They blocked us in the corridor and controlled the stairs with coordinated fire. I wanted to try to reach the stairs from the other side, but to do so, I would have to cross the portion of the corridor below them.

We tried to get closer, but once we reached the corner, several shots exploded between my feet. The same blows that, even today, remain imperishable within the walls of that school. I soon realized that there was no way to climb. The only way was to try a combined attack on two levels.

To implement that precise attack pattern, we would have had to blow up the windows, but we could not use our Breachers.

We heard more shots from outside, and who knows why they were firing at Mariwan. "We are under engagement, there are other terrorists in the houses around your building!"

Great, I thought.

There was confusion in there, and we had to find a way to go upstairs.

We attempted the assault from the stairs. There were two flights, respectively, one on each side of the building. There had to be at least four because when one fired the other, he charged, and, alternating, they always kept a fire on the stairs, which was the only way to access the upper floor. We tried and tried again, but it was impossible, several were injured. I decided to fall back and regroup to attempt a combined two-tier attack.

I left the building and joined the captain who, as always, was on the phone.

"Jassim tell him we can't go up from the inside."

"What are we doing?" he replied

impatiently.

"We have to blow up a window to create an opening on the upper floor and break in, if we assault the two main levels, they will lose the fire domain on the stairs. This is the only way to be able to climb ..."

We found some fire brigade stairs. I intended to blow up a window with an AT4 to create an opening so that the teams would be able to reach the upper floors in coordination with the operators on the ground floor. It was a diversion that would keep the terrorists busy on both levels.

We could handle a combined assault, and that's the only way we could get them out.

"We're in town, we can't use rocket launchers. Are you nuts!? There is too high a margin of error, we risk collateral damage."

Indeed, the captain was right. During operations in the city, it was forbidden to use rocket launchers and explosives of any kind to minimize damage to things and buildings that were in the vicinity of the target. If I had missed the window, the missile would have passed the target to impact who knows where, perhaps in a park or a garden of some house, ending up killing innocent civilians.

I had fired several times with the AT4, always in combat situations, I knew it well and had achieved a good familiarity.

"Captain ... I'll fire! I can hit the window. The missile will land on the window and explode inside ... being at close range it will be an easy shot, let me try ... "

"Alex, I can't risk it! What if there were hostages? "

"Look, I went in there with my men, there are no hostages, we talked to the neighborhood police the school was closed for days, we have been trying unsuccessfully for hours to climb the stairs, and there was no way ... "

"I said no, Alex!"

At that very moment, I did something I never thought I would do in my entire life.

I took the radio out of its case and placed it in his hand.

"You are the captain, do your own thing. I'm out ..."

He looked at me.

"What the hell are you doing?" he scolded me.

"There are two methods. If you want to make it your way, you'll go in there to get them out. If we do it my way, I'll go and lay them down here in front of you before sunset!"

I told Jassim to translate. I would never have allowed myself to disregard an order from my captain, and it would never have occurred to me to speak to him that way, but unfortunately, I did it.

He looked me straight in the eye, shook his head, and took a long sigh.

"You know that if something happens, they'll screw us, do you?"

"I do, captain, I know, but I take all responsibility for it ... tell me ... have I ever disappointed you?"

"No, Alex, you've never disappointed me ... you can proceed ..."

I couldn't believe it. He said yes.

We called everyone out of the structure. Some were attacking the houses where other terrorists were hiding.

I took an AT4 from my Hummer and headed toward the school gate.

"Everyone gets out of there," I shouted. I got down on my knees and told some of the boys to keep their eyes on the windows. I suddenly opened the pointing devices. I removed the safety. It had to be a single shot, I could not go wrong. I charged the firing pin. Now the missile was ready to fire, I would just have to crush the double safety devices, and it would start against the building, opening a hole in the facade.

Everyone was staring at me. I felt like Roberto Baggio at the penalties of the final of the World Championships of Italy in the 90s, but I was firing a missile, not performing a penalty. If I were wrong, there would have been catastrophic consequences.

I looked at the captain, waited for his nod, the teams were ready. Alfa had already placed the ladder, while the second team was ready to enter.

Now he was looking at me, he was serious, he nodded affirmatively. I aligned the front-rear sight with the rear one, opened my mouth slightly to prevent the explosion from stunning me, and pressed the safety catches with my fingers.

The missile did not start immediately, it seemed as if it had misfired, it was not like firing a standard weapon, it had a slight delay. Then the moment came. The shot went off at an incredible speed, I had never engaged targets so close. After the explosion of the launch charge, I did not see the missile go off, but I only discerned the impact on the building facade.

A tremendous cloud of dust rose around me, and at the point of impact, it took a few seconds before I could see the consequences of the shot. Once the dust cleared, the surprise was endless. The window was smashed.

Perfect launch!

All those present went into a stadium

cheer as if I had just scored a goal, some opened fire on the gap.

The teams rushed up the ladder and took their positions outside the destroyed window rousing the raid. I hooked up to the team that would enter from the floor below. We climbed the stairs, fired a Flash-Bang, and continued up and fired. The team above was in, and we had reached the second level. Within minutes we cleaned room by room, throwing explosive grenades to neutralize the occupants. For OP SEC reasons, I will not reveal the methods and information found inside the building, but during the last phase of the operation, one of us was hit by a bullet, fired by one of the occupants.

Once we took control of the building, we went out and left the others to clean up.

Sunset came, and we returned to base. The bodies of the terrorists were taken by civilians, who attacked them on the cars and dragged them all over Kirkuk like grisly trophies.

We never liked these demonstrations, yet civilians cheered us on the streets of Kirkuk, while we gave no signs of jubilation.

We were tired, dirty, bleeding, and we had lost a dear friend, there was absolutely nothing for us to celebrate. We returned to the base exhausted.

The captain gathered the men on the barracks forecourt. As his habit, he gave his speech. We gathered in silence for the victims of the RAID.

He gave me the word, and Jassim translated each letter. I didn't say anything significant. I just thanked everyone and went through the group shaking hands with each soldier saying: "Supas", which means thank you. Finally, the captain released us.

"Stop!" I said to my detachment "you don't ..."

The boys couldn't stand it anymore, they begged me to let them go.

"A few more words guys, then we can go home."

I stared at them, we were totally upset, man.

"You fought well today, I'm proud of you. Let's make sure that the sacrifice of our brothers was not in vain ... "

The group gathered around Aram, weeping over the loss of one of his best friends. I patted him on the shoulder, and he nodded back.

"Why? Why him? " he asked me.

"It's war, my friend ... it's war ..."

I threw myself on the bed, without even taking off my uniform stained with bloody sweat and fell into a deep sleep..

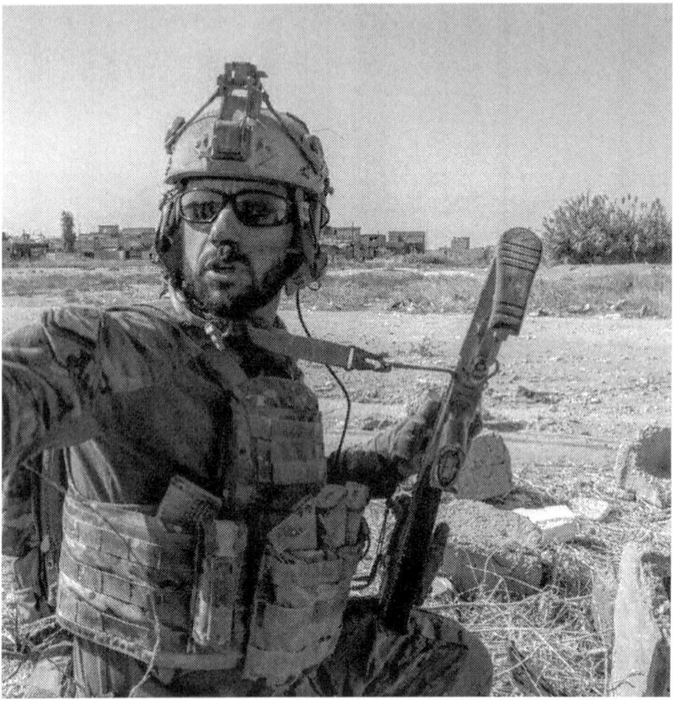

Following that event, the unit split in two. One side had to stay in Kirkuk in case of other attacks, while the other was to continue the Mosul offensive. During my shift phase in Kirkuk, I received the captain's order to go to the school we had just released. The school principal wanted to have a talk with me.

"What have you done?" he said laughing.

"Me? Nothing, Captain. But look, you were there too... "

"Mmm, I think they want you to pay the damages to the school, Soresh ..."

"Damages?"

"Yes, damages, you threw a missile into the school, remember? And you were live on RUDAW[3]."

I couldn't believe it, he meant it.

"How come damages? What about who shot? Are we mocking me?"

"Soresh, don't get mad, go and see what the headmaster tells you, maybe she's hot."

---

[3] Kurdish National TV Channel.

I couldn't understand how this was possible.

When did soldiers start pay damages?

After a few moments, the captain added:

"Get a car and an attendant, go see what she wants. Please, Soresh, be respectful, she is a chief! "

I took a vehicle of ours, and I took Hamad with me to translate my translator. Sebastiano, a cameraman who was shooting a documentary on volunteers in Iraq, also came for the occasion.

We arrived in the neighborhood, in the same place where, a few weeks earlier, the terrorists forced us to attack. We were welcomed by a group of school children who, to my amazement, were different from the one I remembered. A couple of teachers also came out and showed me the location of the chief's office. They didn't seem mad at us for the missile I had launched directly into the top floor window.

"You are Mr. Alex ... aren't you?"

"Yes, I am. Nice to meet you…"

One of the teachers approached, she smiled, shook my hand with respect. I could sense her great strength of mind and her tenacity, she did not wear a veil and had a flute in her pocket.

"Nice to meet you."

The neighborhood where the attack took place was populated by a singular ethnic group, the so-called KAKAY, famous for their strength and determination. The men had a thick mustache, while the women, on the contrary, were of particular beauty, similar to "Gypsy".

They explained to me that Isis had attacked that school, located in that neighborhood because Etna Kakay were not considered good-believing Muslims. They were also accused of being the descendent of an ancient religion: Zoroastrianism, a culture based on the teachings of the prophet Zarathustra. Back in the days, it was the main religion most widespread in the regions between

Iraq and Central Asia between the sixth century BC. and the 10th century AC.

The teacher had around her neck the pendant that represented the dignity of Ahura Mazda, the one who inspired many icons used by the Kurdish people.

"Come, Mr. Alex, the Headmaster wants to talk to you ..."

The teacher accompanied me inside the school. As I crossed the threshold of the door, I noticed how the same scenario, which only a few weeks before had been the scene of death and terror, had become a playground for children. The screams of the little ones with their satchels and aprons filled my heart with joy.

Returning to that school again was a leap into the past, softened, however, by an awakening made up of small refreshments of the kids who ran around behind me, wearing mice behind their piper, looking at me with big eyes full of admiration.

I finally reached the door of what

should have been the Headmaster's office. So I believed, in short, until just before opening the door.

On the other side of the walls, I found the principal together with a whole class of children of different ages. Once inside, they all stood up and greeted me in chorus.

I was amazed, my heart came in my throat, and with it, a wonderful feeling began. Those children were sitting on the same desks used by the terrorists a few days earlier to barricade the doors and windows of the building. I perfectly remembered the door of that classroom, located on the first floor of the building, the same one that was previously imbued with hatred and terror, now bursting with smiley faces and the big eyes of dreaming children, who in their innocence sat on their school desks.

The principal smiled at me and welcomed me:

"Welcome to our School, Mr. Alex! "

Everyone was so nice to me. After a few moments, she added that they were waiting for me and that they had organized a surprise with the help of my captain.

"You, Mr. Alex, have returned the school to our community, and all the children are grateful to you for this ..."

A little girl came up to me with a small plastic seedling. She handed it to me in gratitude. The teachers asked me to give a speech in front of the children, but first I should have reassured them. They told me that some of them thought they could find some terrorists holed up on the upper floors.

I felt so weak and fragile. I had armor, a camouflage suit, and a rifle, yet in the face of that innocence so profound, the warrior in me bent down. I remember stammering a few words trying to give those guys a reason for hope. They would have encountered many difficulties during their journey, but they would never have to run away. They had to fight because, unlike many other children, adolescents raised in other areas of the world, they would surely have a Peshmerga by their side ready to fight for them and die for them.

After years of hard work and training and sacrifice, it was at that moment, at that very moment, that I found the answer to why I had left. Why I wanted so much to fight the terrorists and go to the front lines. The one and the only reason it was worth dying for: those children.

I would have liked every soldier in the world to have the possibility in his existence, even if only for a few moments, to be faced with the result of his battles and sufferings.

After talking to the children and thanking the principal for the wonderful surprise, I left the class, the teacher came up to me crying. She was saying something, but I couldn't understand her, maybe it was a dialect.

"What does she say?" I asked my interpreter.

Hamad stopped, staring into space as if to think. His eyes turned bright.

"You are a Hero, she says you are a Hero Master ..."

In the local culture, there are no honors, the few that are given are granted directly by the authorities for acts of extreme valor or courage to the fighters who perform them.

When the war was over, I received a medal for my service directly from Kurdistan, but nothing meant as much as that word said with tears in her eyes by the teacher of a semi-destroyed school in the middle of the sandy Kirkuk.

I felt a lump in my throat and something climb up my stomach, my eyes became shiny and I could not utter any words, I felt that something had awakened a part of me that for too long had taken refuge who knows where, holed up in a dark part of my soul. At that very moment I understood that I had not lost myself, that I had not become like those I was trying to fight. I looked for a corner where to hide, cautious about not to let any tears fall on the face, cautious not to show signs of weakness to those who called me "Hero", but only with me against the wall of that school I was nobody, I was only myself as the weakness that distinguishes every man.

When people ask me to explain to them the reasons that pushed me to do what I do or why I left everything at home to put my life in danger for people so far from us, I never know what to answer. I often remain speechless without knowing what to say. Words are not enough to describe the flow of emotions that I experienced over those years. I suffered, I enjoyed, and I promised myself to do the right thing, or maybe there is no answer, but that each of us has within ourselves. Many ask me if I would do everything I did again, and the answer is YES, I would do it all again, and I would risk everything again.

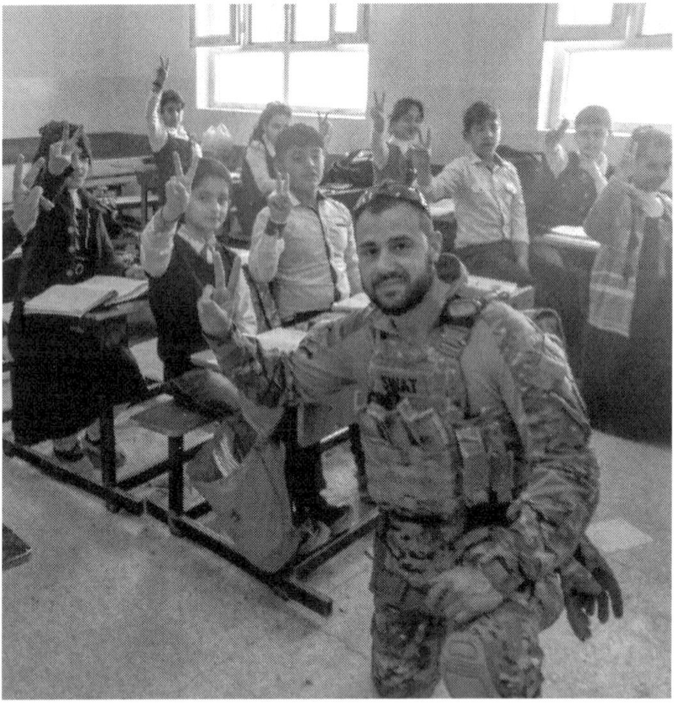

6

THE LITTLE GIRL OF MOSUL

Erbil - October 2016

During a weekend of rest at a friend's place who was hosting me in the Green Zone of Kurdistan, the phone rang.

It was Jassim, my captain's translator. A surreal dialogue began.

"Alex, where are you?"
"In Erbil, Jassim"
"Why in Erbil?"
"How why, I took a few days off"
"And why in Erbil?"
"Why Jassim?"
"Because can't I walk around quietly in Kirkuk".
"Ah, oK. Look, you have to get back to base," he said, laughing with an excited voice.
"Why, do we have something?"
"Let's not talk on the phone, just come

to the base. Captain's order. "

"Okay, are we in a hurry?" I had a service car, and in case of emergency, I had the authorization to use the siren and flashing lights.

"No Alex, there is no rush. But please come, ok? "

"Ok, I'm getting there."

It was a hot time when Iraqi forces were preparing to attack Mosul

Mosul was the capital of the isis, the last stronghold of the Islamic state. A city of six hundred thousand inhabitants.

I remember, even before leaving, I thought about what it would be like to fight in Mosul.

A modern Stalignrado that the militiamen would not have abandoned and would have been willing to defend it inch by inch with the sole purpose of slowing down the advance of the Iraqi troops.

The battle of Mosul was for every soldier something comparable to the Olympics for an athlete.

At the same time, it was a nightmare:

the nightmare of all those who should have entered first.

A large-scale house-to-house battle of close quarters, ambushes, snipers, and hand-to-hand combat. This was to be the battle of Mosul in every soldier's head.

Even before leaving for Iraq, I was thinking about the day I should have entered that mess.

The history books will talk about it, I thought, and I'll be in the pages of those books.

We of the Task Force were calm since the Peshmerga theoretically should not have participated in that operation because Mosul was in Arab and not Kurdish territory, so we were more or less confident that they would not ask us to penetrate the city. With the latest offensive in Kirkuk, the war was supposed to be over for us.

I spent a period as a "guest" on the Kurdish front north of Mosul in charge of surveillance and monitoring. I helped some "friends" setting up an advanced base for data collection and monitoring of enemy activities.

That was the front closest to Mosul, and the fact of being so close to the lion's den, which for years had filled the legends of this war, was almost unreal. I didn't believe it. I was there a few kilometers from the capital of the caliphate, a short distance from the dragon's head, which had remained invisible for years.

I quickly packed my bag, civilian clothes, and my uniform and headed for Kirkuk Road. I could have waited calmly, but the truth was that I was so excited, I thought, I thought ... How will it be? I was trying to repeat in my head the potential operations that could have pinned us down by staring at that strip of asphalt in the middle of the desert.

That evening there was wind, few cars around. Kirkuk Road was a dangerous road often visited by wicked people, especially in the evening. There were checkpoints every twenty-five kilometers, but anything could happen between them. I was driving a car with government signs, the windows were darkened so that no one could see from the outside that I was driving my vehicle alone. When I approached the checkpoints, I lowered the windows letting the light get into the car to be recognized, showing my card. The guard officers at the checkpoint most often reciprocated with a respectful martial salute.

Only high-level officers drive Toyota Land Cruisers and were allowed to have tinted windows which were strictly forbidden for ordinary agents and non-commissioned officers. Even the lieutenants were not allowed to have a service car with dark glass.

I drove with my service pistol under my thigh, I could use it quickly in case other vehicles would approach me. I was always wearing the seat belt, and the airbag had been deactivated to continue driving in the event I had to break through a roadblock.

I could turn off all the lights in the vehicle by pushing just a button. This would let me drive in total darkness using my night vision device, furthermore, my car had a GPS tracker connected to my operations room connected to an alarm switch that I was supposed to use in case of an emergency.

My faithful M4 was always on the passenger side, given the short barrel I could easily swing it inside the vehicle.

On the back was an Evacuation Bag and my Kit

I always traveled like this, alone.

It was damn dangerous for a Westerner to shoot alone in Kirkuk, especially after sunset, but my perception of risk at the time was rather dilated, living every day in the tension of operation. So sooner or later, you adapt, and it becomes your new routine.

After passing the checkpoint of the Erbil governorate, considered the safest area, a cloud of sand rose, which transformed everything into a Martian scenario. The air turned red, the road invisible ... I decided to stop to get out of the vehicle and better observe that wind of sand.

I entered as in a cloud that separated the dimensions, a bubble made of sand and earth that isolated me from the rest of the world, I had a premonition ... as if the desert was telling me something. The desert is such a place where often, without asking questions, you get answers, but that evening what I found was not an answer.

For a moment, I stopped thinking about which mission the Commands were going to give us. It was a nice sandstorm, I thought and enjoyed the show, in a total absence of color.

One thing that still impresses me about Italy today is the variety and brilliance of the colors: every day I lose myself in the number of color tones that our country offers, especially in summer when I drive the road to Portovenere on my old Super Ténéré. The green of the trees that clashes with the blue of the sea and that of the sky.

That's not the case over there.

The Iraq I lived in every day was a country made of the gray of the bricks of the shabby houses, the ochre of the sand turned from the front, the black of the oil on the rocky earth.

The air always smelled of gasoline and was always dirty, it felt like living inside a large refinery, and in fact, Kirkuk was one.

A few grains clashed my face, but it was not annoying. It almost seemed as if the desert wanted to caress me.

What are you trying to tell me? The storm vanished as if to give me an answer.

I got back in the car, convinced that time had stopped inside that space-time bubble. I restarted the engine of my Toyota and drove in silence to Kirkuk's heart.

I reached the driveway, and after the routine check, I entered the base as was customary. I parked my car in front of the officers' command, which at that moment was full of SUVs with government plates. To the side, in the waiting area, some well-equipped men were refreshing themselves. They seemed to be the escort of some big shot visiting my captain.

Even though I was not a senior officer, I was authorized by the Commander to park my vehicle in that parking lot, close to my quarters and sheltered from the pranks of the soldiers. The non-commissioned officers' cars could not enter the base or park near the headquarters.

I went to the captain's office, where I noticed the turmoil from outside.

Jassim saw me, came up to me, and stopped me.

"Wait, don't come in now."

"Quiet. Ok, can we make some tea? "

Jassim looked at me and gave a half-smile, a wry smile like that of a kid who just stole candy.

I stared at him, and I laughed too.

"Jassim ... Tell me everything".

Jassim was not a soldier and had never had any military training. He was the captain's brother and had emigrated to England after the American invasion against Saddam Hussein. He had grown up in the London suburbs acting like a little gangster and probably had been.

During the offensives, he was the captain's attendant, and he was not interested in fighting. He wanted to get his salary and live his life.

In the beginning, we had quite a few problems. He was often arrogant and disrespectful. I remember how he showed up one day in my apartment and ordered me to clean his gun.

Today I smile when thinking about that evening and how irritated I was by that cutting request.

I answered with a laugh and teased him by telling him that there are three things a real man must never let other men touch. His weapon, his motorcycle, and his woman.

I put a toothbrush in his hand and told him he could do it himself.

The conflict continued for a while, marked by small teasing of various kinds until the day I had the opportunity to participate in the operations.

From then on, I had earned his respect

and Jassim became one of my closest friends and allies.

"Tell me Jassim, why are you laughing under your mustaches?" I asked as I poured the boiling water into the cup for my tea.

"I can't tell you," he replied, stirring the sugar with the spoon.

"Come on, you called me on purpose, where are they sending us?" back to Tel Ward? "

"No"

"Okay, shall we begin the Awija offensive? Jassim shook his head.

"So we have operations here in Kirkuk? "

He put the glass of tea and sugar on the table and let himself go in laughter between euphoric and hysterical. I looked at him thinking he was crazy, and I laughed too.

"Hey man, what's that hookah in there?" Jassim and the Captain's General Staff used to hide a hookah in a closet behind the parking lot because it was forbidden to use it inside the base, but everyone knew it.

The office door opened, and a series of uniformed officers entered. They appeared to be some Iraqi military.

The captain for the occasion wore his ceremonial uniform. The thing that made me laugh the most was the ranks. Silver stars on the shoulder pads that compared to ours in the Italian armed forces were enormous. They were silver since TF Black was a military police force, equivalent to our Carabinieri, we could operate both inside and outside the city, unlike the Peshmerga who were not authorized to conduct operations inside the cities.

He used to wear his traditional Kurdish dress, complete with a handmade leather belt, a holster for his Glock 19, and magazine pouches for his M4. He looked like he came straight out of an old black and white photo. He was a good commander of men, and from the few times I have seen him in combat, also a good soldier. He had trained with the Americans during the war against Saddam and was previously an Iraqi army officer. He was his Unit's "father", and I felt him a bit as an Uncle.

He sported a big smile under his mustache, and his face always clean-shaven and groomed. At the end of each briefing, he used to tell me in a good-natured way to cut my beard, which wasn't an option for me, not even under torture. He never gave me any order, but only requests. He always smiled and could instill calm in his men, even during an attack.

I entered the office banging my right foot on the ground, raising my knee well, and waving with my hand to my head. The Kurds have a very different formal education from the Western one, and to learn their formal martial gestures, I had to follow two weeks of training at one of their official schools. I was often wrong with a mix of Western and Kurdish formal education, and this made my senior officers smile.

I remember that even if I was not formally required to follow the rules, whenever I entered his office, the captain got up from his chair and returned the greeting with a smile and a handshake followed by the word that defines the end of formalities.

DANISHA

Sit down

"Yes, sir," I replied.

Tea always followed. It didn't matter if you didn't want it or said no ... if the captain tells you to drink tea, you have to drink it.

It was served by Ali, one of the captain's attendants who had only the assignment to make tea. In Kurdish culture, every commanding officer of units has a dedicated attendant just for tea, and it was the best tea you could drink in Kirkuk.

I was eager to know. In the room with me were Lieutenant Mariwan, who was also my support and point of reference before the captain, and Lieutenant Mohammed, both commanders of the Alpha and Bravo platoons. My detachment the DELTA was smaller in number than the platoons of Mariwan and Mohammed, but it was much better equipped. My detachment was considered an extension of platoons A and B, and in special cases, it could be of support to the other units.

After a thousand battles with the Command, I had managed to have a sort of "independence" that allowed us to operate under the practical control of the two Platoon commanders but isolated from the rest of the group.

I had obtained "special" funds directly from the captain, we wore different uniforms than the rest of the unit, and I had selected and trained the volunteers who wanted to join the DELTA detachment. It was no coincidence that my detachment took the name DELTA. The boys liked it because it reminded them of the legendary American unit, the DELTA FORCE. The reason for this name was simple: the unit was organized into three groups, Alfa and Bravo rotated for seven days at the base and seven at home respectively, then there was the

Charlie group which was under the command of Sergeant Major Hussein.

The platoon Charlie had mainly logistical duties, including the base siren and escort services. My detachment took the name of DELTA and was divided respectively into D1 and D2 with rotations of seven days at the base and seven at home, each team was commanded by sergeants major, who were also my subordinate.

I enjoyed a certain amount of independence regarding training and operations. I could receive the instructions directly from the captain or the two commanding officers of the detachment in case of support for their TASK FORCE.

I let the tea cool as it had been poured at a temperature that would have burned the palate. I had learned the traditional way of drinking tea and showed it off during the lounges and meetings, unleashing the sympathy of those present.

I poured the boiling liquid onto the

saucer under the cup and casually brought the plate to my mouth. I repeated the operation several times: every important meeting is preceded by the tinkling of the spoons that turn the sugar inside the glass cups where that mystical drink was served.

With this background, in the silence of his office, he said to me with a straight face:

"How are your boys, Alex?"

"They're ready, captain". I had my technique with the captain. I never asked for anything before he asked me to do something. I always needed more means and resources both on a practical and administrative level. He preceded me. "Do you need something for yourself or your boys?"

This sentence left me speechless. There were very few cases in which he offered me the opportunity to ask for something. I was perplexed and met the eyes of the two officers who nervously toyed with their pens and their notebooks in hand. I had in mind a long list of things that my boys and I were missing, and they were all important things, but I opted for one of the priorities.

"Captain," I replied with dutiful respect, "the windows of our Hummers are broken, we have already hit the windows during the last offensives, and I'm afraid they won't take any more impacts."

"I know Shoresh, we have all the glass of the armored vehicles cracked, look at the glass of my Suburban jeep ..."

"Yes, sir, I see it".

"Is there anything else, Soresh?"

"Yes, captain, many of the radios in my equipment are damaged. I can no longer guarantee internal and external team communications, we often have communication problems, and it is difficult for me to coordinate with Lieutenants Mariwan and Mohammed." The captain nodded:

"Have you already applied for it?"

"Sir, yes sir, several times".

"And..?"

"Nothing, the radios are always the

same. Sir, I have already forwarded all the requests to the administrative office, but I have not received any response yet. I took the liberty of buying some of the items I still have the bill. If it were possible to get refunds, that would be great."

He scolded me: "I already told you you don't have to spend your money on your team's equipment. Why did you do it?"

"I did it because, without that equipment, it would be impossible for me to operate. "

He grunted irritably.

"Let me have the receipts, and I'll try to get you back for the material you took. "

He raised his eyes and looked at me seriously.

"We are going to attack Mosul. "

"Mosul? "I answered surprised," isn't that the Iraqis' business? "

"Yes, but our leaders want us, Peshmerga, to clear the way to the outskirts of the city, and from there, the Iraqi Special Forces and Federal Police will penetrate the city."

During the offensives, the pattern was

almost always the same. An army assault force and a military police unit would open the front, and we, as military police units, had the duty of opening the offensives together with the assault military units. We were employed as a light infantry unit that could move easily within the villages and outskirts of the cities controlled by terrorists, and we were often asked to carry out the close defense of tanks and vehicles that broke through the terrorist lines.

Mosul was no exception.

"I await orders, captain, we are ready," the other two lieutenants confirmed the same.

"Perfect!" He exclaimed slamming his hands on his wooden-colored plastic desk.

"For now, don't say anything to your men, just call all the staff back to the base. We will open the Kurdish offensive in Mosul, and Task Force Black will have its piece of history. "

He dismissed us, and in order of seniority, the officers left the office repeating the formal greeting on leaving. My turn came, and the captain stopped me with a gesture and pointed to the chair.

"Sit down, Alex"

"Sir, yes sir"

"How long have you been here with us?" "

"It's been almost three years now, captain"

"Three years" he repeated "it seems to me yesterday that you arrived," he said smiling "you looked like a chick ... you know? "

"Yes, Captain. I remember it." The captain nodded slowly.

"You fought with us, you trained our men, you are one of us, Alex ..."

"Yes, Captain, thank you, I'm honored for this"

"Look, you know, you don't have to fight? "

"Yes, I know Captain, I've never felt compelled to Fight," the captain lowered his voice and spoke the words more slowly.

"You know that if you don't want to, you can easily stay at the base"

"Captain, what are you trying to tell me?" be honest with me "

"Alex, we appreciate that you are here with us and the men are happy to be commanders of you, they trust you, you give them courage, but I must repeat to you that no one here is asking you to come with us to risk your life and that if you decide to do so, you will assume all the responsibilities of the case "

"Captain, I am aware that no one is forcing me to participate in the operations. It is my choice. and I do it voluntarily. "

"Excellent, I have here a sheet that I ask you to sign, where you declare your willingness to participate in this Offensive as a volunteer in support of the Kurdish forces, relieving any responsibility from the Command in case you are wounded or killed during the operations. As you can see, it is written in English so that you can understand. "

"Captain, I have already signed such a

declaration, why should I sign a new one?"

"This time it's different, it's Mosul." There was an awkward silence for a few seconds, and I looked at that paper that had come out from somewhere and rested on the desk. I took the pen.

"Okay Captain, I'll sign."

I left the office saying goodbye, pondering on what I had just signed. It was an indemnity, a discharge of responsibility of the Command in case I was injured in action or the worst case I would die ... There it is, I thought the Kurds just want to protect themselves from a hypothetical diplomatic "nuisance"

Having signed that paper brought me back to reality for a moment.

I was neither one of them nor one of mine ... I was thus in diplomatic limbo, without a legislative position, without a certainty of what would happen to me when I returned home, sure no flag would ever wrap my grave if I ever had one.

I carried the flag of Iraqi Kurdistan on my arm, but inside the left pocket of my uniform, I was hiding an Italian flag which I could not display for obvious security reasons. I always carried it with me.

Although I served in the ranks of the Kurds, since it was them who materially fought that evil called ISIS, I never stopped fighting and defending not only for my homeland but also for the whole of humanity.

I always believed that the more we eliminated them, the less they would arrive at my house.

I was a soldier without a flag, a mercenary, a traitor, they said on my return ...

Words that hurt me more than bullets.

The offensive began, we crossed the vast territories of Kurdistan to reach the gathering area of the troops ready to attack.

We walked the Kirkuk Road armed on our matte black vehicles, and the panthers drawn on our vehicles roared in the direction of the road we traveled. We left our areas of jurisdiction behind. They no longer mattered. The political divisions between the Kurds, the Iraqis, the jurisdiction ... everything had vanished. All dissolved in forming a single large block that united those who were divided, with the sole purpose of falling now to the Capital of Evil.

Units from all over Iraq joined the block by surrounding rural areas around Mosul to leave no escape for the jihadists.

Volunteers from all over the world came from afar to participate in that historic battle.

Amid that block made up of fighters from every corner of the globe, I was also convinced that I wanted to write a few words of that story.

The asphalt flowed under my feet, and my mind scanned these words like a mantra: We will win, we will free Mosul from isis, now you are Alex, now you are part of history.

On the way, many civilians and

refugees gathered in the streets to celebrate the troops.

We loaded our Hummers onto the trailers and sat on them.

The civilians on the sides of the stride shouted phrases like "Er Biji Peshmerga" Long life to the Peshmerga. The displaced people clinging to the nets of the refugee camps shouted in Arabic: "Go and take back our homes", "kill them all".

We passed a factory of chips and other various crap. Some workers went out and threw some boxes full of potato chips on the trailer, and the soldiers pounced on the gifts of civilians like grasshoppers, gulping down the fonzies of an unknown sub-brand produced in Kurdistan with who knows what nutritional quality parameters.

Accompanying that improvised appetizer, there were always the "TIGERs" of which the Peshmerga were greedy. A kind of Redbull duplicate that smells of chewing gum chewed by a camel, which was then declared illegal by the Ministry of Iraqi healthcare.

I, out of camaraderie, joined in and grabbed a packet of potato chips thrown in my face by Sergeant Salar. It doesn't matter what it is, but if it's free, you must get it! This is what tradition dictates. I stuffed a couple of fries in my mouth and gulped down some of that terrifying drink created with the worst preservatives, amid the shouts of joy from the soldiers. A burst of burps accompanied our journey for a few kilometers towards the most decisive battle in the war on terrorism.

We arrived in the troop assembly area in the evening, exhausted after hours of travel on the back of a trailer with nostrils full of dust and the breath that smelled of Iraqi fonzies. We unloaded our armored vehicles and got ready to receive orders around 2 am in the Iraqi desert, twenty kilometers away from the urban center of Mosul.

The flames of the burning villages rose in the distance into the night, emanating the smell of burning rubber.

The captain called the assembled platoon by platoon and ordered Attention! I gave Attention to my detachment. He showed up with an envelope full of Iraqi dinars, and one by one, he called the names of the soldiers.

It was a kind of donation consisting of 35,000 dinars, the correspondent to about twenty-six euros, a kind of gift from the Command. I premise that the boys at the time, due to the crisis, had not received any salary for about five months.

Everyone worked second jobs, and many had problems at home. For this, they agreed to pay this money into a common fund at the platoon level and use it for the families of the fallen in the battle that was to be there in a few hours.

Later on, the captain distributed additional weapons and ammunition. Each soldier received two hand grenades in addition to those already in his possession. Each Hummer received two AT4 rocket launchers, as well as other material I won't mention for OP-SEC reasons.

Our mission was simple: penetrate the five villages that represented our goals and secure them.

The terrain was desert without the possibility of counting on a cover in case of approaching the targets. They would let us in, and then once inside the village, they would start with ambushes and booby traps.

The jihadists who remained in those villages knew very well that they would never return home. Their only purpose was to die carrying as many "Kafirs" (infidels) as possible.

I ordered my fellows to sleep and get ready for the order to move, but for the whole evening, the Coalition Aviation gave its fireworks display, hitting the targets we would have penetrated after the bombing ended.

We established advanced observation points to examine any movement in the villages.

ISIS knew our technology very well and had devised tricks that were as simple as effective to evade it.

A few tires had been placed on the sides of the main streets of the urban teachings and had been set on fire to create tongues of fire to turn the night vision goggles into useless tools. At night we observed the movements of vehicles using thermal chambers as the engine was the source of heat that left the vehicle to be detected in the night. But moving through these flaming streets on the sides made us unable to detect any movement too because we were blinded by the fire.

The bombings were no guarantee that we would not find any surprises upon our arrival in the village. The militiamen of the Islamic State had built a dense network of underground tunnels and bunkers precisely to evade the potential of the Coalition bombs. There was even talk of a real underground structure.

At the first light of dawn, the drones flying over the targets were helpless to see anything because of the hood of smoke that covered the villages. A pitch-black smoke coming from the fire generated by the tires, and the air was unbreathable and stank. If I spit on the ground, it would seem like I was spitting oil. The troops were started. We had studied our goals on digital maps and had planned our operation all night. We opted for an arrow attack formation with ALFA on the right side, BRAVO on the left side, and DELTA in the center. Maintaining the alignment would have been a problem. My goal was to act as a bridge between the two officers who made the formation wings in front of us. With the task of breaking through the front, there was the 70th Brigade. An excellent infantry brigade was also equipped with some heavily armored vehicles. The plan was more or less this.

Brigade 70 with its bulldozers and thought-out vehicles would have acted as a breakthrough as the first wave, while Alfa and Bravo would have protected the flanks of the formation from any attempts to bypass. With my detachment, I would have acted as a backup to the boys of the 70 who had the task of opening the way for us until they arrived near the inhabited center.

From then on, my detachment and I specialized in urban guerrilla tactics would have penetrated the village intending to acquire some altitude points that we would have used as a position for the snipers and machine gunners of the 70 who would, in turn, cover the advance in the deep.

Ok, you might say the perfect plan, but I'm sorry to disappoint you ... that plan was far to be perfect.

The order to move was given after a few hundred meters. The vehicles in line following the bulldozers, which used to open the road, began the maneuvers between the dust and the roar of the engines. In my Hummer, the air was hot and dusty, visibility was poor, and I couldn't see anything that was further a couple of meters around my vehicle.

During the maneuvers, the boys of the 70 began their tactical movement. The explosion shook the earth and raised a cloud of dust that blinded us ... Then another explosion and then another and another ...

The offensive had begun.

The militiamen threw some VBIEDs, or armored cars packed with explosives that crashed into the opening vehicles of the 70, at us and it was chaos.

The .50 machine gunners opened fire in the direction of the village, aiming at random.

"Team DELTA, ceasefire!!!" I shouted on the radio to Salar, who was in charge of repeating my orders in Kurdish to the rest of the platoon.

The ringing in my ears muffled every noise and disoriented me. The dust prevented me from breathing and between coughs I gave the order to my commrades to dismount, take the rocket launchers, and prepare to counter the suicide attack waves.

The boys got out of the vehicles backing up their rocket launchers and waited for the next VBIED. Something came out of an opening amid the dust, pointed at us, and headed toward us. The machine guns hit it, but they were unable to stop it. If that mass of iron and death reached our positions, it would kill us all.

I jumped aboard a pick-up to gain some altitude and raised the sights of my rocket launcher, removed the safety mechanisms, and took aim. I fired my AT4 at the vehicle that was approaching my formation. The rocket went off so fast that I lost sight of it immediately.

There was a roar, a whistle, and then yet another explosion. I hit the vehicle and it smashed into a thousand pieces, throwing splinters all around its position. The explosion was gargantuan. I don't know if you've ever blown something up with a rocket launcher, but doing it while saving the lives of the people next to you is priceless. Truly.

The formation fell apart in its first moments of contact with the enemy. We had already been in combat and to us, it was nothing new.

The first wave of The 70 was cut down by suicide attacks. We rushed to help and saw the men torn to pieces. Many were bleeding and others were torn apart by the explosions. Some volunteer doctors and I immediately gathered to save as many lives as possible. I was not a doctor, but I had some experience in rescue. Countless times during this war, I had put my hands inside the torn flesh of the dying human in front of me. At that moment, I was dealing with a boy who must have been about twenty-five years old. Those in the 70 were all young and well trained by a good leader. It broke my heart to see them torn apart, their fellow soldiers wounded, rolling their eyes as if they were looking for God. They screamed, distorted in the pain of their wounds caused by the splinters. Some of them had shreds of flesh ripped from their bodies and were trembling in shock convulsions.

After them, it would be up to us and, if the enemy hadn't anticipated the training, my men and I would be torn to shreds for our comrades.

Thus, the most important offensive of the war opened for me and my men.

We marched for miles in the desert,

approaching the villages razed to the ground by the night bombs. The sun was now high and the heat was suffocating. We entered the villages approaching Mosul. Some lost their lives fighting, others died in ambushes. As we approached the cities, the civil fighting became more and more bloody. The ISIS snipers were killing from afar, not sparing women and children runaway.

We did not sleep for days and days in an attempt to steal as much territory as possible from the jihadist fury.

I survived and maybe one day, I will tell you in detail what it was like for me to go to the devil's house in an attempt to drive him out of hell.

I believe that Mosul was one of the bloodiest and most violent battles in modern military history, especially because innocent civilians, forced by ISIS to stay in the city during the fighting, were paying the highest price so the coalition forces could use aviation without generating collateral damage.

My most striking suffering of the war

was not losing friends. It was not risking death, but it was the evil and pain that I had to see on the skin of the innocent. That suffering that still torments me in certain moments. Then you swallow it all down, without worrying that sooner or later, everything will come to the surface.

I did it, but I promised myself that I would never go back there. Never again.

Meaning and Purpose, By Diane Hanna

"We don't stop being a fighter, we just choose another war." Alex Pineschi, 2021

War isn't selective in who it adversely affects both physically and emotionally. Death, torture, rape and sexual violence, malnutrition, illness, and physical disability include the most extreme of it's physical consequences. Whereas, depression, anxiety, grief, and post-traumatic stress disorder (PTSD) are perhaps best considered part of the psychological legacy it leaves behind. As a result, many well-intentioned clinical Westerners all too often operate on an assumption model, using tools and methodologies to try and alleviate pain and suffering, whilst ignoring cultural and religious coping strategies. From the outset, I was determined not to be of of those people and instead learn from the experience as it unfolded.

When I arrived as the first psychologist on the mission in Mosul I held no clinical assumptions about my wider role as a psychologist for the surgical trauma team, and instead decided to let the situation itself inform me of such. As it turned out, one of my best teachers, charged with the task of securing the hospital, was Alex Pineschi. Quite and unassuming at first, often tapping away on his lap top in the operations room and peeking up from behind his screen I had figured him to be I.T at first. But, after offering him some coffee on my first morning and pulling up a chair with him for less than thirty minutes, I left the room a hell of a lot better informed before entering it and as a veteran, I got his humour as well.

After my chat with Alex that first day, I decided that my role would be a hybrid one, where I liaised between security and the trauma team, while also providing one on one psychological assistance to the surgeons and staff. One of Alex's main responsibilities was to check the ambulances for suicide bombers and other hidden dangers compliments of ISIS, despite the heightened and at times desperate sense of urgency by those wounded and suffering inside. Among the casualties were often cases of unaccompanied minors, children without any adult or care giver to protect them. The risks these children faced included a myriad of unthinkable atrocities, such as forced marriage, child labour, trafficking, and more. Whether orphaned due to death, forced displacement, or some other instance of familial separation, Alex and his team would assist me in locating any living relatives and help get them to the compound if possible. All children were vulnerable, perhaps suffering the most being subjected to such unprecedented violence and sheer brutality. Their scars of war in particular had the power to make grown men cry as well as the most hardened of psychologists.

It was when I saw him with the children, that I noticed Alex's rugged exterior often betrayed him giving away a much guarded level of tenderness toward them. Like many of those in law enforcement or other related fields, we tend to over emphasis the importance of keeping our objectivity to keep our head in the game. But what we risk is failing to keep that connectivity to all that keeps us grounded and our humanity which put us on this type of particular road in the first place. Whether he was passing out the odd armful of chocolates on the roadside to them, or simply posing with them making the victory sign with their hands for a selfie, you could tell that this man was on a mission to make the world a better place. Our conversations between in-coming ambulances would often focus on the frustrations that had been barriers for us back in our homelands. He had finished giving me a thick description one day about his experiences in greater detail to which I simply nodded and replied, "Meaning and purpose." For certain types of people, meaning and purpose is their oxygen, and without it they die inside. With Alex, I could clearly tell which category he was in from the very beginning.

Together, we would work toward polishing the policies and procedures around casualties and their discharge, or death, and devise ways that were operationally viable and appropriate given the circumstances, although some didn't seem exactly fair. For example, we devised a fifteen minute visiting roster, where one visitor at a time was escorted onto the ward, and returned to the main gate fifteen minutes later, where the next visitor would be waiting their turn. While this minimised the level of risk inside the compound, we witnessed their angst from beyond the main gate. How to choose who went first? One time, Alex and his team had all pitched in and organised for a local farmer and his beat up utility to help someone with their deceased relative's body, as there were strictly no provisions in place for such.

Instances where the surgical trauma team had tried tirelessly to save the lives of those brought in only to see them pass away before their very eyes, required a disclosure to the family or friends, waiting outside the main gate, which became one of my main duties. As a psychologist with many years experience this task never gets any easier. One of my first debriefings with a family back in Australia was a sobering one. The two daughters had accompanied their parents in my office at the medical centre, among the sterility of blue privacy curtains, rubbing alcohol aroma, and the desk between us all. As both girls wept on the parent's laps in from of me, and their father spoke stoically about how proud he had made him feel despite his son believing otherwise before the incident, I struggled hard to maintain my composure. It wasn't any different out in the middle of the Iraqi sunburnt desert either. The first time I had to inform a man that his brother had died during surgery was incredibly difficult. He had been waiting so patiently, with his heart still bursting full of hope, and as he saw me walk toward him he smiled and began to say something in Arabic. I didn't want him to start the dialog, because then it would have been too difficult to halt. He didn't seem to sense anything other than positive news from me which was all the more gut wrenching, and thats when I looked at Salah, to alert him to translate for me. I uttered the words that sealed off his hope forever, and with that he fell to his knees onto the stones below him. It wouldn't be the last time I had to do this.

The backdrop of shared suffering on such a grand scale magnified and intensified the senselessness of it all. Unlike the family in Australia, there would be no funeral service, because there was no cemetery. ISIS had even destroyed that too. What made this disclosure harder was the fact that I had been informed that we had ran out of body bags that morning and that the staff were trying to organise something. From memory the body was wrapped in a white sheet, before his brother could take him back through the main gate which had became a repository for grief and loss, assaulted and marred at least every few hours by the ambulances which just kept coming. Between the chaos and confusion, Alex had managed to locate the brother of a 14 year old female patient. She had been inconsolable after they had became separated while fleeing the conflict. As she lay wounded in the bed, she had drawn me a picture of two roses, and a heart which was pierced with an arrow, depicting universal love, and perhaps the hope that they would both be reunited again soon. I entered the ward the following morning, after receiving a call from the nurses to find then together. Her brother was a 16 year old boy, and he was sitting beside her bed now holding her hand. I smiled at them, and caught a glimpse of Alex in the background through the window behind them. He was once again making his way back out along the muddy laneway of the compound with his trusty M4.

Through our experiences in Mosul, and a sense of deep validation and respect for one another, Alex and I forged a tight bond and I knew that I would be a better person by having met him. After my rotation ended, I returned to Australia for three months before I knew I had to go back. Most Westerners will tell you how the place gets under your skin, and for all it's physical characteristics of a place on a map, there's an intangibility to it that drives you on to commit to the process if just to be a small part of the overall effort made there. I later returned twice on two other missions, during 2017 and 2018, with MSF - Doctors Without Borders, and ACF - Action Contre La Faim, as the mental health activity manager as well as mental health care practices manager addressing the psycho-social aspects of malnutrition. Despite the abrupt closure of my project in Hamman al Alil, I chose to stay on in Iraq, and work in a local hospital for a year, before my accident which I am still slowly recovering from.

Each day we have on this earth is a chance to do it all over again. I've always believed in having no regrets, as long as I know my heart has been in the right place. If you don't know your meaning and purpose, it's time to find it, never believe that nine to five is all there is. Once you stop living your life for others or the life you believe you need to portray to the critical audience that just sits inside your head, you will truly be free to get on with the stuff that matters to you most. The people I met in Mosul will live on in my memory for as long as I draw breath. They are the ones who will help me choose another war. As for Alex, he will forever be one of the most influential and important people in my life. I remain eternally thankful for his protection, advice and education, as well as grateful for an enduring friendship that I will forever cherish.

Mosul Field Hospital

In reality, the exact opposite of what I imagined took place. Months after the end of the first attack, I found myself still fighting in that hell.

Protecting a hospital field was one of the toughest psychological challenges I have ever faced during the war, but I have never been so honored to serve on that project.

We stood guard at the hospital field. Our task was to ensure the security of the perimeter and accesses. ISIS had already attacked some hospitals using ambulances loaded with explosives.

It was a delicate task with no rest, in contact with the threat of blowing up and the screams of pain of the wounded. The cries of their loved ones. During the Mosul offensive, many arrived, mostly civilians and children.

Isis, now clearly defeated, was giving its last swings by launching suicide attacks using brutal and infamous guerrilla techniques.

I have seen their snipers shoot children to avoid civilians escaping from areas they control. I have seen them shoot pregnant women for the sole purpose of scattering psychological terror.

I have seen them use ambulances full of explosives and explosive belts to attack hospitals.

We were there to defend that hospital.

I deeply felt the responsibility of the assignment because we were protecting the doctors who were working to save innocent civilians.

We were the filter between the outside and the entrance to the emergency room.

We had to stop every vehicle, keep it at a distance, search it, and avoid any attacks on the facility, a very high-value target for the terrorists.

Every time a vehicle approached, we felt the tension rise…. If it didn't stop at a halt or if it proceeded at too high of a speed, we would have had to open fire to stop it. I could never forgive myself for a mistake, but it was often extremely difficult to understand who or what was approaching and thank God we never misjudged. My biggest fear was killing innocent people by mistake.

We not only dealt with that, but we often lent a hand to the doctors managing the wounded. We helped out the relatives of the victims. It was an excruciating job. I was the team leader of the detachment and I was in charge of the entire management of the field security system as well as the operativity.

Nights and days no longer existed. I slept at intervals every six hours. There was no room in the doctors' quarters, so we made do with some containers.

When injured people arrived, intoxicated by chemical weapons gases, we all had to wear personal protective equipment. We wore heavy, thick rubber suits with gas masks and we had to put all the equipment on top of it to fight. It was a hard job, but both the guys and I felt important and that's why we did it better.

It was a hot and muddy afternoon because it had rained and the whole area was a swamp. A high-speed pick-up truck arrived and, as always, we ordered him to stop, pointing our weapons at him. If he went through the first barrier, we would open fire.

I caught up with him, scanning the vehicle, observing the driver, and telling him that he had to put his hands in plain sight outside the window. We carried out the procedure, the driver in tears shouted, "I beg you! Let me pass. They are dying!"

I heard that sentence every day, but reluctantly, I could not afford to check them too quickly. ISIS could stage an emergency to get past the gate and blow up inside the hospital.

I reached the chest and in a pool of blood I saw a little girl, about four or five years old at most, with both legs partially torn. Some rags were wrapped around what was left of them. Beside her was the broken body of an adult. Possibly her father.

I was dying inside because I knew how important a few seconds can be to manage bleeding, but we followed the procedure. We checked the van. We searched the driver and rummaged among the bodies, looking for any weapons or explosives. It was frustrating, but we had to follow the procedure. Being a civilian vehicle, it was not allowed to enter, so I took that little body in my arms, her legs dangling, and ran to the emergency room. The doctors were busy amid the screams of patients on the couches. I entered screaming to attract attention.

One of the doctors looked at me. I shouldn't have gone in there without authorization.

"Please, excuse me, but do something," I pleaded to a doctor.

The little girl died shortly after.

I went back to my seat amid the silence of my men.

"Let's get back to position," I said. I wanted to cry, but commanders never cry.

"Alex, go change. I'm here," Kastro, my subordinate, told me. He put his hand on my shoulder. "You're covered in blood. Don't let yourself be seen at the entrance like that."

I went to my makeshift accommodation, where there was no running water. I wiped the blood off the gun with a rag, which I soaked in a puddle. I changed my shirt and I went back to my seat.

Shortly after, another pick-up arrived, heading toward the base. Same procedure. A woman with desperate eyes got out and asked for a girl and a man who had arrived in a van shortly before. With her was a boy probably about the same age as the girl. Her little brother, perhaps.

We all looked at each other, aware of the news that this woman would soon receive. I ordered Kastro to continue the procedure with the new vehicle and ask the woman to go into the waiting tent.

I gave that order sharply without letting any emotion pass through, but it was as if a thousand knives were piercing my heart.

We called the doctor, who sent a psychologist who, inside the tent, lying on the mud, gave him the news of the death of her daughter and her husband.

I publish with her permission the drawing of Diana, an Australian psychologist who worked at the United Nations hospital in Mosul. She had a passion for drawing, and shortly before leaving, she gave me this drawing she made, the witness of that umpteenth tragic event.

That woman lost her mind. She dragged herself, tearing her hair in the middle of that damned swamp, screaming all her pain and shouting at us.

We stood still in position.

Sitting on the ground was the child. He didn't cry. He watched everything that happened sitting in a puddle with wide eyes. I don't think he was able to understand what was going on. With the crazy mother, the dead father, and the big sister killed by a bomb.

We looked at each other again. Our eyes turned sad as the balaclavas covered our grimaces of pain. The little brother remained motionless in a state of catalepsy. I pulled down my balaclava. I approached. I took him out of the puddle and I took him into my arms. He weighed little, like his sister.

"Zain?" I said in Arabic. Well?

He looked into my eyes, unable to hold back. He burst into tears in my arms. He cried so hard he couldn't breathe. Cried so deeply that he spasmed. Again, a thousand more knives were in my heart.

It was not a cry. It was the voice of pure pain. He despaired until he was sick, aware that he had lost everything.

I looked at Kastro for help.

"Who did this?" he asked the child, who replied shouting with a piercing voice, "Daesh! Daesh!" He leaned his head against my flak jacket, continuing to shout and curse that name. I held him and I could hear the hatred in his screams.

Another ambulance was approaching. We had to get back to our locations

Before leaving him again, he looked at my rifle and raised his eyes, touching my M4, and said something. He whispered it and repeated it several times.

"What did he say?" I asked Kastro.

Kastro looked at me through his balaclava, changed his gaze to "combat" mode, and, staring into the boy's eyes, he said, "Kill them all. He told you you have to kill them all…"

I was silent.

The radio crackled.

"Vehicle approaching, team in

position."

"Roger," I replied.

7

CONCLUSION

You see, this is how it works. War often leaves no room for feelings. You can neither cry nor suffer. Your brain tells you that you will think about it later on because right now, you have a duty to obey and you cannot leave any space for feelings. You would risk compromising your function and the more responsibility you have, the less you can concede yourself the luxury of suffering.

The brain is an extraordinary machine that adapts to the most distressing situations. War is continuous exposure to suffering and the human body, just like a perfect machine, adapts to the environment. There is just one purpose–surviving.

During the war in Iraq, I put together my friends' torn bodies, staining my hands with their blood. I saw innocent people die violently and brutally before my eyes, unable to help them. I observed human madness and its capacity to generate terror and devastation. I have seen abuse, torture, and malfeasance.

I shouldn't have felt anything. No anger, no pain, no sadness. I could only have chosen to act and put an end to that suffering once and for all, turning discouragement into motivation.

I know that many of you will not understand the reasons that made me stay there for five long years. I didn't want to leave until that evil was eradicated. If my mind would not be strong enough to cushion all of this, perhaps I would have gone mad.

The mind adapts and when it perceives external stimuli that could compromise the body functionality, it activates strategies to preserve it. Imagine the brain as a sort of command station and when the emotions sector is overwhelmed by millions of emotional bullets, the brain command station protects the whole system. It decides to disconnect the whole unit. It is as if, all of a sudden, the feelings switch has been moved to the

OFF position. You no longer feel anything. You no longer perceive anything.

Any respectable warrior cannot claim to know himself until he pushes himself to his limits, even if only for a single moment. There, inside my cell in the trenches of no one's land in the dust of the desert, I often had time to think. I was thinking about what my limit was. Not much about the physical ones, because heat, hunger, thirst, and fatigue can exhaust the body, I can relate to it, but war destroys the mind day after day, gradually, without you realizing it, constantly stirring you toward decay.

How much suffering will I have to endure still? How much more evil will my eyes be able to observe? To what extent will my mind be able to handle all this? This constant, daily exposure to evil, brutality, and suffering.

I said to myself, "Alex, a little longer. Resist a little longer. You can still hold up!" But how long can I hold up?

The only way not to lose your mind is

to believe in it. You have to believe in it fully. So, what's at the end? Well, simply there is nothing. That is it. No emotion, no suffering. Once you go beyond your limits, nothing remains. Just total emptiness. You will find yourself being impassive to all the evil you will be exposed to daily.

The body, as well as the mind, is a perfect machine and it will try to protect and preserve itself to remain functional. Once we reach our limit, we become impassive. We have a job to do and we cannot afford to jeopardize our functioning, so the mind does what it takes to preserve our mental integrity. It deactivates emotions and closes all the suffering we are exposed to in a drawer at the bottom of our soul. Everything we feel will stay down there, in that drawer, until it is time to go home. Then the drawer of memories, of the most profound emotions, will open again. We will find ourselves facing a new enemy that is invisible and harmful. The demons of war will awaken every night. They will be there, ready to bring the memory of a time spent in those trenches in blood and pain back to us.

Anyone who decides to give their life for a cause similar to the one I did must understand one thing: This choice will change your life forever. War takes away a part of you. A part of your soul. You will never be the same person again. But I don't want to talk just about the dark side of war.

In battle, I have seen simple people perform heroic acts. Men and women helping others. Even among the scariest evils, there can still be good.

I have seen people who, despite having lost everything, continued to give to others without expecting anything in return. Sometimes I smile when people ask me, "You mean you didn't take any money? Did you fight voluntarily?" Most people don't do anything for nothing. They try to get something out of it eventually.

Maybe, when you hit rock bottom and lose everything, you understand how much you have to offer the world.

Now, when I can, I set off on my old motorcycle in search of something that one day I may find. I walk the road, trying to give a bit of serenity back to the world. Some say I am running away from something. Perhaps from the past. But that is not the case. During my travels, I have seen the good that people have to offer. Maybe I am looking for that. After seeing so much suffering, I think I travel in search of happiness.

The war showed me the worst side of humanity, but at the same time, it allowed me to get the best out of life.

War is that place where you come out understanding who you are.

I thought a lot before writing this book. Years have passed and the writing itself was an adventure. I didn't know whether to divulge such personal stories, but after a long time, I made up my mind and put my thoughts together, omitting some details for the safety of myself and those who still serve the cause there today. I told my war story, but also the stories of those who were part of it, on the field and from home.

I told of Kirkuk, of the Peshmerga, and of how people managed not to bow to evil. I talked about the men who have made a huge difference in my life and those who sacrificed their lives not just for their country, but for all of us.

I did it. I went home, but I changed. Yes, I've changed now that I understand how important life is.

Coming home was not easy, especially at the beginning. I was overwhelmed by discouragement. I didn't have a group, a department, a regiment, or my fellow soldiers to refer to. I have often felt very lonely and disoriented, to the point of not feeling at home at all.

My sleep was always haunted. I could never sleep peacefully. I woke up every day more tired than before, afraid of having lost everything I had built. Of no longer having a goal in life, unsure of what I would do without the security of a future. It was hard to come back and it still is now, but I realized how important it is to live not only for us, but for the people around us who love us and out of respect for those who didn't make it. Those who have not had the opportunity to live the life that we are lucky enough to be able to savor every day. For those we have seen fall in battle without being able to do anything about it.

I know friends that it hurts, every day and every night, but it is our life, the path we have chosen, and we must live it as best we can.

Often when I am down, I cheer myself up by thinking of what I have done. That I have survived everything I have seen in battle. Because of it, I can now face anything that will come to my path without the tiniest hint of fear.

Don't let the past ruin your present and future. I've been through all of this, but I'm still here. By following a few simple rules, I tried to make sense of my life when I returned home. These are the same principles that I want to share with you.

8

THE TEN RULES

Rule number 1: Find a goal and pursue it with determination. It is vital to give yourself a reason for living. Look for a mission, whatever it is.

Rule number 2: Plan every move in detail. Be organized and disciplined, as in battle. Organize your spaces in a systematic way. It will help you to think clearly and efficiently.

Rule number 3: Don't give up. Always be determined!

Rule number 4: Follow a routine and keep to it with discipline.

Rule number 5: Do the deadlift. It is important to take some time for yourself. Have fun, laugh, go around, dance, and above all, travel. In short, do anything that does not conflict with the other rules, but find the time and resources for yourself to regenerate.

Rule number 6: Surround yourself with people who truly love you. Learn to distance yourself from negative people. Gradually get closer to those who can give you something and stay away from those who always have others in their mouths. Stay away from those who do nothing but look at others and guide the actions of others, since one day they will do the same with you. Don't let the judgment of others become your reality.

Rule number 7: Don't expect others to understand you. They won't. They weren't there with you and they didn't live your experiences, so how can you expect them to be able to understand you? Don't feel sorry for yourself. Your problems are yours and nobody else's. You alone have the key to solving them.

Rule number 8: Recognize your

limitations and work to overcome them, but at the same time, if you have already done everything you can, accept them with discipline and use them to your advantage.

Rule number 9: Try to serve your neighbor. Bring the same principles into civil life. Be honorable, defend the weak, keep your word, and do not be vindictive.

Rule number 10: I'll let you write rule number ten on the last page of this book.

I don't have the solution in my pocket. Often, they are a more total landslide, so take these words as personal considerations. Thank you for spending your time reading a part of my story.
I hope you can treasure it.

My rule number 10:

ACKNOWLEDGMENTS

Thanks to all those warriors who fight a silent war against terrorism, crime, and the evil that afflicts our society away from the spotlight and in the silence of the night. To all those who have paid the price for their courage and dedication to protect others with their lives. To the veterans wounded in the flesh and the soul who fight every day to return to life. To all those volunteers and fighters whose names no one will ever know, fallen and injured in the war against ISIS to protect humanity.

Thanks to those who gave me a chance and who gave me friendship without expecting anything in return. Thanks to the students of my school (AP TAC) who have always supported me (and also bore). Thanks to those who give me a chance to start over but above all, thanks to those by my side in the most important battle of this life.

A special thank you goes to those who worked on this writing and to *you*, who spent your time reading my story.

Finally, thanks to all the Peshmergas everywhere, to all those who have decided to be "in front of death" to defend their neighbors.

THANK YOU

Alex Pineschi

GLOSSARY

AT4 anti-tank rocket

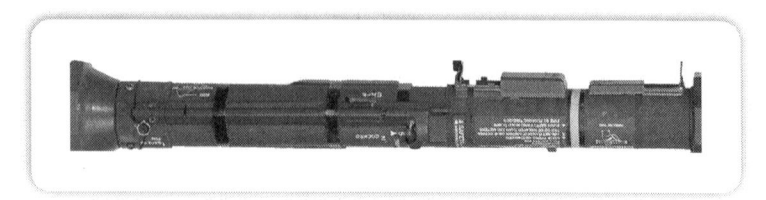

Disposable shoulderable anti-tank weapon equipped with launcher tube and unguided rocket with 84mm anti-tank warhead. Produced by the Swedish Bofors and operational since 1987.

Weight: 8kg

Length: 102 cm

Maximum effective range: 300 meters

AK47 Kalashnikov assault rifle (and derivatives)

This abbreviation generically identifies an entire family of assault rifles chambered for Soviet 7.62x39 ammunition and derived from the original design by Mikhail Kalashnikov of 1949. There is no official statistic, but it is probably the most widespread assault rifle in the world. It is popular for its versatility and toughness on the battlefield.

M4 carbine (and derivatives)

Compact version of the Colt M16A2 chambered for 5.56 NATO ammunition. Operation with direct gas removal and with burst fire capability. Extremely versatile weapon system. It can be equipped with various additional devices (aiming systems, aiming lasers, tactical lights, etc... etc ..). The first operational version was presented in 1994 and, over the years, has undergone numerous redesigns to overcome some original technical problems. Currently, the ergonomic configuration of the weapon has been taken up by various gun manufacturers who market proprietary versions.

3rd generation monocular night vision / PVS14

Passive intensification monocle, 3rd generation battery operated. On the market since 2000, it can be used as a hand-held monocle, mounted on a weapon, or, more commonly, integrated onto a combat helmet. Powered by a single AA battery and weighing approximately 350g. It has a 40 ° field of view and an intensification gain of 3000 fl / fc. With ideal night conditions, it has a range of 300 meters concerning the recognition of a human silhouette.

AN / PEQ15 illuminator and laser pointer

Aiming aid for long weapons based on visible and infrared lasers (to be used in conjunction with night vision goggles).

PKM machine gun

Machine gun chambered for 7,62x54mmR ammunition in production since 1969. Gas recovery operation and open bolt. Produced in various versions and barrel lengths, it has seen action in practically all modern conflicts and is appreciated for its extreme reliability and robustness.

Waypoint

In a planned route places can be identified on the map with coordinates or other methods (geographic references on the ground distinguishable). These references, used as "control points" to verify that you are on the correct path, are called waypoints.

Infrared Laser (IR)

A laser can be defined as a device that emits a beam of coherent light at a certain frequency. One of the advantages of laser beams is that they remain focused without dispersion, even at great distances. The beam can be emitted on visible frequencies (eg red and/or green) or in frequencies in the infrared spectrum (abbreviated IR, in fact), and therefore invisible to the human eye. The typical application of the IR laser is that of an occult aiming system, both night and day. An IR laser beam can only be detected by devices capable of working on compatible frequencies such as night vision goggles.

Flash-Bang Grenade

A non-lethal pyrotechnic device is used as a tactical diversion. This is a grenade capable of generating multiple bursts of considerable sound intensity and blinding magnesium flashes.

Breacher and Halligan Tool

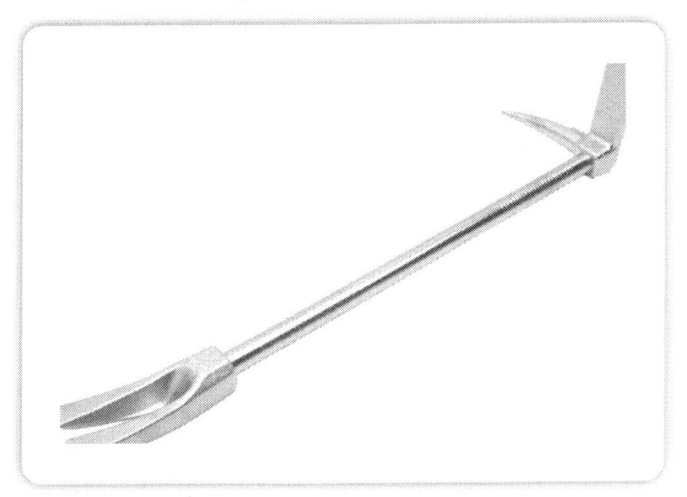

The breacher is that component of an intervention team who has the task of removing all obstacles that arise during the advance. In an urban environment, typically, its task is to violate fixtures, such as doors and windows, and/or create breaches in the walls. It usually uses mechanical methods and impact and cutting tools, such as but not limited to breakthrough rams, axes, cutters, hammers, crowbars. In the most extreme cases, it can use explosive charges suitable for the purpose. A Halligan tool is a tool used by the breacher to perform the actions described above. Initially designed for firefighters, they have also become popular in military/law enforcement.

Caliber .50 BMG (12.7mmx99)

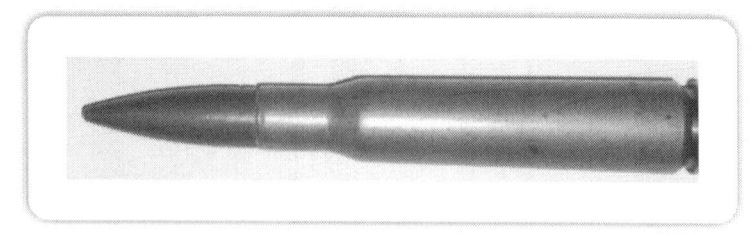

Massive ammunition was developed in 1921 for the Browning M2 heavy machine gun for anti-aircraft and anti-vehicle use. Over the decades, a worthy replacement in terms of ammunition has never been found for the engagement of targets in an anti-material function, or the remote destruction of radio installations, light vehicles, and the like. Over the years, several shooting platforms have been developed (including the famous M82A1 Barrett rifle and successful models), to give a very long-range sniper connotation to the ammunition. In modern conflicts, ammunition is used as a form of light artillery against urban targets due to its excellent ability to pierce walls and armor. The ammunition is produced in various versions, including tracer, incendiary, explosive, armor-piercing.

CQB Close Quarter Battle

Set of tactical procedures and combat techniques with engagement distances from zero to one hundred meters. Usually, there is a tendency to identify combat activities inside buildings with this acronym. Not to be confused with the activities of MOUT - Military Operations in Urbanized Terrain - Operations in an urban environment of which the CQB is only a component.

Rendez Vous

Literally "meeting point." In military jargon, we mean a pre-established physical place where to converge.

Stick IR - Chemical lights

Containers of various sizes, usually cylindrical, made of transparent semi-rigid plastic. They contain two liquids separated by a small diaphragm. By deforming the container until the diaphragm breaks, the liquids mix, triggering a cold chemical reaction that results in light on a precise frequency. They are on the market in various sizes, colors, duration, and light intensity. They are commonly called Cyalume from the name of the first company that invented them. They are available in all colors of the visible and even infrared spectrum.

Military Grid Reference System (MGRS) geographic coordinate system

Geographic coordinate reference system used in NATO.

Rocket Propelled Grenade (RPG)

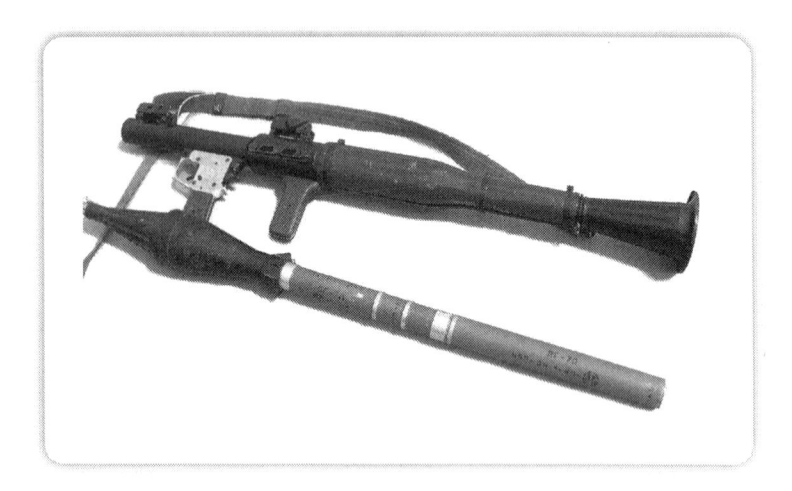

A shoulder-mounted weapon with a reusable launcher tube and an anti-tank rocket. A solution made famous by the Soviet versions that have made multiple versions with warheads adaptable to the tactical situation.

IED -VBIED

Respectively Improvised Explosive Device and Vehicle Borne Improvised Explosive Device (car bomb). These two abbreviations identify a whole category of homemade / improvised explosive devices used for unconventional guerrilla actions. A typical example of IED is the use of an unexploded artillery shell that is camouflaged under a road and detonated as the target passes by with circumstance trigger systems.

Printed by Amazon Italia Logistica S.r.l.
Torrazza Piemonte (TO), Italy